TRIANGLE

Three Novellas of Ireland

For Mary

Pól Ó Muirí

TRIANGLE

Three Novellas of Ireland

Triangle

is published in 2022 by
ARLEN HOUSE
42 Grange Abbey Road
Baldoyle
Dublin D13 A0F3
Ireland
arlenhouse@gmail.com
www.arlenhouse.ie

978–1–85132–287–9, paperback

Distributed internationally by
SYRACUSE UNIVERSITY PRESS
621 Skytop Road, Suite 110
Syracuse, NY 13244–5290
United States of America
Email: supress@syr.edu

Typesetting by Arlen House

cover painting by Amy Flaherty
is reproduced courtesy of the artist

LOTTERY FUNDED

Contents

7 *Acknowledgements*

13 This Project

49 Elizabeth Éilís

71 Father Monsignor

100 *About the Author*

ACKNOWLEDGEMENTS

The author wishes to thank the Arts Council of Northern Ireland for a grant given under the Supporting the Individual Artist Programme. Without it, this work would not have been undertaken.

'For every species of beast and bird, of reptile and sea creature, can be tamed and has been tamed by the human species, but no one can tame the tongue – a restless evil, full of deadly poison. With it we bless the Lord and Father, and with it we curse those who are made in the likeness of God. From the same mouth comes blessing and cursing. My brothers and sisters this ought not to be so.'

– James 3:7–11.

'That same evening, at a certain aristocratic club in Dawson Street, Dublin, five or six gentlemen were in the smoking room, discussing the papers and the world news. They had met after luncheon for business; and the nature of the business might be guessed from a sheaf of telegrams that had been sent at five o'clock over the country and to the great landlord clubs and centres in the cities. The telegrams were brief: No purchase. No abatement. Bide time.

Six words, which in a month's time carried desolation into many a Munster and Connemara cabin.'

– Canon Patrick Sheehan, *Lisheen* (1907)

THIS PROJECT

It was the price of the watch that finally did for me. 'How much did that cost?' my grandfather asked when he caught sight of my new luxury watch. I lifted my hand up a little, just so that he could get a better look at it. 'Oh,' I said casually, 'just under five thousand.' I had expected him to gasp in amazement and envy, but he just said quietly, 'That's a lot of money just to tell the time' and went back to reading his paper.

The line stayed with me for the rest of the day. That's a lot of money just to tell the time. That's a lot of money just to tell the time. That's a lot of money just to tell the time. I had half hoped to tell him why I had bought the watch; to be able to tell him that I was doing well in the American software corporation, but I did not have the time. 'My Career' was on the up and, as a result, the amount of time I had to spend with family and friends was on the down. I looked at the watch – that's a lot of money just to tell the time – and decided, petulantly, that I had to go back to the office.

This time my grandfather looked up from his paper. 'But you have just got here. What's your hurry?'

'I'm sorry but it is work. It is one of those places that is just twenty-four-seven. The Yanks don't do Irish time,' I said. 'I'll get back to you later in the week.'

'Twenty-four-seven?' grandfather said. 'What does that mean?'

But I was already on my way out the door, throwing another glance at the watch – that's a lot of money just to tell the time – and did not have the time to explain the Americanism to him. I could feel the tension rise as I headed for the car. I needed to be there soon, I needed to be at my desk, I needed my supervisor to see me at my desk. I did not actually need to be at my desk as my work was well under control but I needed to be seen to be at my desk, seen to be looking to work, seen to be productive, seen to be a loyal team player, seen to be an enthusiastic Yank drone.

The car was new and expensive – that's a lot of money just to drive you somewhere – and I did not need to spend as much on it as I had. But I was trying to impress a girl with the watch – that's a lot of money just to tell the time – and with the car – that's a lot of money to drive you somewhere – and the suits – that's a lot of money for some clothes. I was making money, and I was spending it just as quickly on designer goods. I had, for the first time ever, recently gone in to Brown Thomas to buy some male grooming products – that's a lot of money for some shaving foam – and had bought a designer wallet – that's a lot of money to keep your money in – a very expensive pair of Italian-made shoes – that's a lot of money to walk in – and after that I had gone and bought a designer suit – that's a lot of money for some clothes.

I could feel my parents' disapproval all the while. 'Sure McKenna's do lovely suits? Italian leather shoes? Are Italian cows more pampered than Irish ones?'

Dunnes had been enough for them for clothes and Graham's for shoes. They never had enough money for anything else. I had money though. I was the first of my kind to have money and lots of it. Yank money, Yank money earned in Ireland, Yank money that came from the Yank company that had set up shop to enjoy a generous discount on their corporation tax. They got to avoid paying a fortune in tax and threw us a few crumbs in our salary. Of course, we did not understand that we were getting the crumbs at the time. We did not care. It was money; they had it and we wanted it. We doffed the cap and put out our hands and they dropped pennies into our palms and we became, without realising it, king of the beggars, beggars with degrees.

My father loved my car at first glance, but his mood changed quickly when he saw how new it was. 'Did you pay full price for this?' he asked concerned.

I could not avoid answering 'Yes.'

He shook his head. 'How many times did I tell you never to buy a car brand new? You lost money the moment you drove it off the forecourt. Always get a car a year old and give it a good once over. A year-old car is as good as a new car if it has been well looked after. And even if it hasn't, you can take it down to Earley's and let them have a look at it. They can do anything, those boys. They will save you a fortune.'

I nodded, sighed and bit the bullet. 'It comes with a warranty and is handier for me. I don't want to be driving out of the city to take it to Earley's. Anyway, I doubt that they would be able to do much with this. There are some state-of-the-art computers in this engine. It is not the sort of thing that the grease monkeys in Earley's could handle.'

It was just an excuse. I was not going anywhere near the Earleys and their second-hand Fords and Nissans.

My father gave me a dirty look. 'The Earleys are good people. Many is the one around here who got a good deal from the Earleys. And they know their engines. There is nothing they could not fix. More is the pity that the young fellow could not have stayed at home with them and carried on the work. It is just the father and eldest left now. I told you before if you shop local ...'

He did not finish the sentence. He saw I was not listening to the Gospel according to Saint Father. He gave me a dirty look again. I could see he was becoming angry. Here comes a tantrum, I thought, here comes a lesson on social solidarity and sticking together and looking out for each other and wearing the parish jersey. Here comes the shop steward's talk to his railway workers.

'Ach,' he said. The words choked in his mouth. 'It is a lovely car. Health to enjoy.' He left it at that.

I wish I could enjoy it. I passed Earley's garage on the way to the main road. Séamus saw me and raised his arm in salute and surprise. I returned his greeting with a beep on the horn and a loud 'All the best!' out of the half-opened window. I headed east towards the city, navigated the sharp bends and narrow roads until, finally, the main road appeared. Usually this was when you could put your foot down. Not today. Today there was a long queue in front of me. I cursed. The new road was being built. I had forgotten that. I should have looped around past Hamill's dairy and out the back road into the city but I had wanted to let the car loose for a while.

I sat in the traffic jam reading the roadside signs. 'This project is funded by the European Union.' We all liked the European Union; the European Union was building us roads for free, miles and miles of motorway for free. Soon, the whole country would be linked by free motorway. My father was one of the few not enamoured with it; he loved his railways, but not many others did. 'They can concrete over the whole of Kildare,' I said, 'if it gets me into the city quicker.' The European Union was throwing money at us like there was no tomorrow. Free roads, we thought, what is so terrible about that? 'Nothing is ever free,' my father said – a lesson he had learned as a shop steward. I rolled my eyes. The queue moved ever so slightly. I got the car from first to third gear before having to stop again. There was no chance I would get this into high gear. 'This project is funded by the European Union' I cursed. The European Union was going to make me late for work and the Yanks would not be happy.

I wanted to impress her; I wanted Lucia to notice me; I wanted her to stop and ask me, 'Where did you get those lovely shoes? What aftershave is that you are wearing? What time is it? Will you give me a lift in your beautiful car? Would you like to sleep with me? Would you? Would you like to sleep with a beautiful Italian girl? I want to sleep with you. Of course, I do. How could I not? That is why I am here, to sleep with a 'andsome Irish man.'

It was all to impress Lucia. I was not going to be happy marrying Sinéad from the GAA club. I was not going to stand at the sidelines shouting on the local team anymore. No, I was going to Florence to be married. I was going to be different. I was going to turn my back on muddy Irish fields and soft potatoes for Tuscan hills and pasta, cooked *al dente*. I was going to turn my back on hurling for golf, on Guinness for Peroni, on greyhounds for horses. I would be free as no other Irish man of my age had ever been free. I had a career, not the 'good job' that my parents had hoped for themselves and their children, but a career like you saw on the television. 'Get a good job. Get a good job.' I had done better than that – I had gotten a job with the Americans and their computers that were going to change the world and make everyone rich.

'I am in on the ground floor,' I had said to my grandfather.

'What does that mean?' he asked, 'have you an office on the ground floor? Is that it?'

'No,' I said, 'I am one of the first that they have taken on. You know, it is like when you started out on the trains, helping out, then they let you shovel coal, and then you became a driver. It is like that. I am one of the first to get in. Computers are going to be big, very big. You wait and see.'

'Computers,' he said, 'what do they do?'

'They can do things that we can't,' I said, 'They are the new technology. Global, you know, they will be everywhere and I am working for one of the big American companies. It is big money – by Irish standards. Big money.'

'Computers?'

'Don't worry, granda,' I said, 'It is a good job. And I am in at the start. It is good money.'

'Well, that is something. Good money is something.'

Yes, that was something. I had more than the good job, more than the hope of a bit of overtime at the weekend. I was master of my own destiny. I had studied hard, put in the long hours and got the dream job with the American corporation. I was going to hold on for all I was worth. I would take them for every penny I could get. They would not know what hit them. I would show them what I could do.

That was where I had met Lucia. We were both in the same section. She sat beside me one day, elegant and quiet. I was unsure whether to introduce myself with a handshake, so I just nodded. She nodded back and smiled. The others drifted in. The Americans made us stand up and introduce ourselves in person. The ones from the continent stood up confidently and spoke fluently in English about who they were and what they had achieved. There was Tim and Gretta from Amsterdam, Birgitte from Copenhagan, Lucia from Florence, Michael from Norway, Sven from Sweden, Clara from Piacenza, Sullivan from Cork and Sinéad from Dundalk. We were the only three Irish people in our section. In truth, there were not many of us in the company. I was the first of the Irish to speak. I muttered something about school and university, looked at the floor in panic, sat down suddenly. Sinéad stood. She was confident and beautiful; their equal. Her little speech was funny and well-received. The Americans laughed and clapped when she finished. Sullivan too lacked no confidence. I disliked him immediately. He had set his eyes on Lucia from the off too. She had no sooner begun working with us than he was telling everyone, 'That's the woman I am going to marry.'

I laughed at him behind his back. What a dick, talking like that.

Yet, I had never met anyone as confident in herself as Lucia. She was well-healed and used to the attention of men. She knew her value, whereas I was gauche and unsure of myself. She drew men in with smiles and little, delicate kisses to either cheek. It was cosmopolitan. After a while she began to let us go out with her on little European dates – Sullivan had an interest in the horses and he took her to Punchestown. I kicked myself. I should have thought of that. Sven from Sweden played golf with her; Tim was a great swimmer and took her to the pool. I was last to get any attention. I was too Irish. I did not swim well, did not golf and had no interest in horses. My idea of relaxing was a couple of pints and a match on the television. Sophisticated I was not. The Christian Brothers had not taught me about the finer things in life, about wine or art or how to woo Florentine women. They had taught me how to work and how to work hard. 'Get to university,' Brother M had said in between teaching us irregular verbs, 'get to university and the world will be your oyster.'

They did not care what we studied at university as long as we went to university. They offered us Irish, French, German, Spanish, Italian, Latin, Religion, Maths, Physics, Chemistry, English, Geography, History and Art. They offered us, without us realising it, the world. Our part of the deal was to shut up in class, to keep the head down, to pass exams and to get on. They did not teach us about women, though. We gawped at the female teachers in secret and wondered who they were. We nodded, awkwardly, at the girls from across the road. They laughed, moving on like a colourful flock of birds. We knew them from Mass, saw them at the GAA club, watched them play camogie and, bit by bit, courted embarrassingly, 'Would you fancy going to ...?'

You knew, within seconds, by their expression what the answer to the whispered question would be. A glance to the ground was never a good sign. But, if you had asked discreetly, there would be no witnesses to your failure.

I knew how to read a novel and write a report on it. I knew how to count in Irish and English. The Brothers had taught me languages, but all I could remember was how to say the Hail Mary in Irish, French and Italian. But the hard work got me to university and it got me a degree and I stood there one day, the first of my kind, my mother in her Sunday best, my father in his only suit wearing his non-funeral tie, and me, in my first suit, my university certificate clutched to my chest. The first of my kind.

I might have had to take my learning across to the States, that was where the work was, but the Americans came to us. I got a job at home. Well, in the city. 'You can commute,' my father had said. He listed the train timetable to me. 'It is a good service, that one.'

No, I said, I will stay in the city. It makes more sense.

'The rent in the city is terrible,' my mother said. 'You can come home again. You know you can.'

No, I said, I will stay in the city. It makes more sense.

They were disappointed with my decision; the city was foreign to them. They could have forgiven me going to the States or to Britain, because there was no alternative. That was understandable, but to continue to live in the city when you could come home was incomprehensible. Worse, it was a betrayal.

'Well, whatever suits you best,' my mother said sourly and left to make some tea.

It was that little smattering of Italian that got me in with Lucia. She asked me something one day and I replied with my schoolboy Italian. She smiled, replied and said, 'We should go for a coffee and have a chat sometime.' She looked around, her dark eyes scanning for eavesdroppers, 'Things here are so busy. We have not had a chance to talk.'

'Yes, we should. Things are so busy. You know, if you wanted, we could go to the cinema.'

I had jumped in, instinctively. There was no one around; there were no witnesses should she cast her eyes to the ground and decline.

'A yes, I have nothing to do Saturday night,' she said.

'Oh, that's handy,' I said, unsure.

That night we walked across O'Connell Bridge and she said, 'I saw that film in Italy. The actor who plays the part of the baby is very well known. He is very funny.'

My heart sank, 'You should have said you had seen it and we could have gone to something else.'

'It is fine,' she said.

I slipped my hand into hers. She did not refuse it and gave a little sly smile. I remembered the touch of her palm on mine, and we walked on, hand-in-hand. There was a full moon over the Liffey and it was one of those nights in Dublin when you felt that, finally, finally, we had got it right. Finally, we were a proper European city, and the famine had come to an end. The streets were teeming with young people, the pubs choked with drinkers, and we had money the likes of which our parents could not have imagined. The joy did not last. We stood in a queue on the banks of the Liffey waiting for a taxi to take us home. I could feel her impatience growing. She was not used to waiting for anything. 'This would not happen at home,' she said and I decided I would have to buy a car.

I had gotten it wrong, of course. It was not a date. She kissed me lightly on both cheeks at her house and sent me home alone in the taxi. I had misread the signs; I had not been granted full membership in the union yet. I had not, it seemed, fulfilled all the necessary criteria. The affection shown was of no consequence to Lucia. I went to hold her hand again during lunch the following day, but she just smiled sadly.

'I don't understand,' I said, 'I thought ...'

Sullivan arrived in with a basket full of food. 'Look, Lucia, I got some things from the Italian deli. I thought we could go out for a picnic on the grass.'

'Yes,' she said, 'that would be lovely. We will all go.'

Sullivan looked at me with hatred. I thought about going with them, and spoiling the day for him. It was the Irish thing to do.

'Thanks,' I said, 'but I have tons to do. You go on.'

Lucia smiled again and left with Sullivan; his hand snaked across the small of her back. She did not refuse his touch. I could hear him talking about olive oil and bread, 'I just love dipping bread in olive oil, don't you?'

I nearly shouted after him that he was an idiot and that the only thing that the Irish put on their bread was butter.

Sullivan did not get the girl immediately, however. She went out with Tim for a while. Tim had a girlfriend, but Lucia broke them up.

'Why?' I asked. 'You could go out with anyone? You could go out with me?'

She shrugged. 'It's complicated. His girlfriend is threatening to do things ...'

'To herself?'

She shrugged again, indifferent to the fate of Tim's girlfriend. Lucia had won and Tim's girlfriend had lost. That was the way of the world.

'Because of you? Or before?' I pressed on. 'I thought there was some sort of unwritten rule about girls not going out with other girls' boyfriends?'

She shrugged once more, unhappy that I was asking her questions. That was one of her rules; you did not ask her questions; you simply agreed with what she wanted. The continental ways were not the same as the Irish ways. In truth, I did not care. I just wanted to sleep with her. I wanted to be sophisticated, and that was the quickest way, to sleep with the beautiful Italian woman and that would free me from Old Ireland. I would lie back, naked, with her by my side and I would be free of priest and penance. However, I did not understand the rules. The home rules were, 'How far can I go, Father?' but I sensed that these did not apply to her. My other physical interactions had been based on a shared knowledge of what was and was not acceptable. There were limits, boundaries, unspoken, rarely crossed without explicit permission. Lucia had different rules. What was considered the ultimate reward and intimacy, but rarely surrendered by my Irish girlfriends – few as they were – was available from Lucia. That much was clear from the start. She had taken, or had let Sven the Swede, take her home one night. There had been none of the negotiations with which I was familiar. It had been a transaction of no consequence. I thought that Sven the Swede would now pursue her. He did not.

'You don't understand yet, do you?' he said to me, later. 'This place is full of beautiful women? Do you see them?'

He spoke to me like I was a child, yet we were the same age.

'Yes,' I said hesitantly. I was Irish; we did not hug or talk about our feelings.

'I had her. She is beautiful. The weekend was enough for me. She is very, what is the word, grabby?'

'Grabby?' I gasped, 'in bed, you mean?'

He laughed. 'No! No! Not in bed. As a person. She is grabby. She grabs things. She is not really interested in anything that is not of value. She is not spiritual, you know. Which is fine by me. I was just curious, you know. She was just curious. The weekend was enough. Why would I tie myself down? Do you see Birgitte from Copenhagen? Do you think she is more beautiful or less beautiful?'

'The same, I think, as beautiful.'

'Physically? Really?' He seemed surprised by my reaction. 'Come on, man,' he said, 'no one is listening. She is much more beautiful than Lucia.'

'She has nicer breasts, bigger,' I whispered.

'Yes, exactly. Lucia is beautiful, but not just *basta*!' He held his two hands up furtively to his chest to illustrate his point and laughed at his own joke. I smiled. *Basta*, yes, enough.

The news about Lucia and Tim spread quickly around the office. I could see the other women were not impressed, but whether it was because she had broken Tim up with his girlfriend, or because they had not had the chance to do the same, I was not sure. The other Italian girl in the office, Clara, did not like Lucia at all. They rarely talked outside of work and never socialised. 'She is a bitch,' Clara had told Sinéad, the only Irish woman in the office. 'A stuck-up biiiiitch. You know she had a guy back in Italy? She dumped him once she came here. She used him for years. His family are very well off, but now she has a better job here than she would ever have there. She did not need him anymore, so, you know, *ciao, ciao*!'

I almost laughed out loud. Her pronunciation of bitch had been so musical, 'Biiittccchh', but she had noticed something I had not. I wanted to ask her more, but she was in a rush, raised her hand and gave a little wave. *Ciao, ciao!*

I watched Lucia even more closely from then. What had I missed? What were the rules for European integration? How much money and energy did one have to spend to complete the project? What did you have to surrender to get what you wanted? What was in it for her and, more importantly, for me? I wanted to sleep with her. It was the European thing to do.

Tim and Lucia did get along, for a while, but Tim hated the work more than I did. His real interest was the poetry of Séamus Heaney which he could quote verbatim. He was, in truth, a good bloke. We spent a night in each other's company in the pubs in Temple Bar. He had come with Lucia, while I had been there with Sinéad and the small Irish contingent from the other sections in the company. We had been lamenting Toto Schillaci's goal in Sicily; he had overheard us and drifted into our company. His English was faultless and we did not even know how to say 'Hello' in Dutch. 'I saw Cruyff play,' he said after a while. We laughed, 'You're a liar?'

'No, no, honest to God.'

We laughed again. Honest to God. He had our inflection down pat. He laughed too, understanding the joke.

'In the Netherlands when I was a child. Just before he left Ajax for Barcelona. We all knew how good he was then. I saw him at a couple of internationals too. Unbelieveable control and speed. The television does not do him justice. When you saw him live, you knew, just knew that he was world class.'

'We could have done with a Cruyff in Italy,' I said, 'we play football like stacks of potatoes.'

'Schillaci!' said Sinéad, 'he stabbed us in the back.' She sipped from her drink. 'But that is what Italians do best.'

I am not sure if she was talking to me or Tim. The conversation stalled.

'How are you finding the work?' I asked him.

'I hate it,' he said, 'hate it. It destroys my soul.'

Sinéad and I blinked. 'Really?' I said, 'That is what I thought too! But it is good money.'

'Yes, I suppose, but so boring. I only took the job because I wanted to see Ireland.'

'Why? There is nothing here.'

'Do you not like poetry? I like Heaney. I thought I would come and see the places that inspired him. Heaney is good.'

'The Cruyff of poetry,' I joked. The most I knew of Heaney was a couple of lines from 'Digging' but Tim had found something in the lines which I had not.

'Yes,' said Tim, 'that is good. I will use that in my thesis.'

'You are doing a thesis?'

'Just an MA at UCD. It is a taught one, but we have to write a short thesis. It is a good course. The work, you know, it is so boring.'

I nodded into my drink. Christ, I could not have faced another exam. And poetry? Christ, he did actually think we were poetic?

Lucia drifted back. She nodded to me, smiled and ignored Sinéad. Sinéad, to her credit, ignored her back. Sinéad had nothing to worry about. She was as beautiful as Lucia, but not as calculating. The men in the office stood in awe of her red curly hair and green eyes. 'She is like something from a fairy tale,' Sven the Swede had said. If she was, there was no happy ending in it for him. Sinéad was not for giving up her pot of gold to any Viking raider.

Lucia had obviously decided that she was not going to be bothered with Sinéad. Lucia did not bother too much with any of the women at work; it was the men who ran after her and she enjoyed and encouraged that. She did not want other women interfering with her flirting.

'Let us go,' she said to Tim.

'Now? We were just talking about the football.'

She sighed, 'I have to go in tomorrow.'

'It is Saturday,' I said.

'Yes, but there is something I want to finish up.'

The conversation stalled. She offered no explanation as to what it was.

'Alright,' said Tim, 'we will go.'

Lucia kissed me gently on both cheeks. 'I will see you Monday.'

She nodded coolly at Sinéad. Sinéad faked a smile.

'She is a wagon,' said Sinéad, when she left, 'a total wagon.'

I did not reply and Sinéad left to join her friends. 'You are wasting your time,' she said to me. I looked at the ground. I should go into the office tomorrow too, I thought. Lucia will be alone. I can talk to her. She might be impressed by my work ethic. I spent Saturday in the office. She did not appear.

I hate this work. I hate every moment of it. My grandfather and father worked on the railways. They drove and repaired trains. They have hands of mahogany, hard and salted by proper work. My hands are soft and white. I get paper cuts. I spend my life in front of a screen, typing like a eunuch. The work comes, I process it, it is sent on, more work comes, I repeat the process. The money is good. I have a career. The work comes, I process it, it is sent on and more work comes, I repeat the process. Think of the money. Think of the money. Tim is right. There is no poetry in this. None. There is nothing tangible in it. My grandfather and father drove trains. They took people from one place to another. They talked to people. They helped people. Their work was hard but worthwhile. They did a day's work and went home. I never go home. I never finish work. There is always more work. We are expected to be always working. We are expected to be at our screens. We are expected to be happy. We are Americans now. The shift never ends. Work never ends. Computers are the future. I am the first of my kind to have a degree. Think of the money. I live in the city. I pay rent to a landlord. We all pay rent to a landlord. I have a career. The Americans have come to us. We are not poor. We are the first of our kind not to be poor. Do what the Americans say. Follow their example. Work! Work! Work! Stay at your desk. Work! I hate this work. It is without value. It is boring. It is useless. Stay at your desk. If you stay long enough, you will get shares in the company. You will be the first of your kind to have shares. Stay at your desk. Lucia will want you more if you have shares. Lucia likes things. Lucia is grabby.

'He is not doing well?' I said.

My father sighed. 'No, he is not. Prepare yourself for bad news.' His voice catches; we both know this is the end. I feel tears in my eyes. I love my grandfather. He has always been kind to me, yet I have not seen him in many months because of my work. My father rang me in the end. 'You had better come home and say your goodbyes.'

'Is it that bad?'

'Yes.'

'Things are difficult here at the moment. I have a lot on,' I said. 'I will come down at the weekend. I promise.'

My promise was worth nothing. I had promised before.

My father paused. I could feel the tantrum rise. He paused again. 'I will let you know if he gets any worse.' He hung up. I went back to the screen.

Now we are standing looking out over the half-built motorway. It is night, but the motorway is lit and they are still working.

'I am amazed that they are working at this time,' I say quietly.

My father pauses, deciding whether to speak to me or shout at me. He speaks. 'They are under pressure to get it completed for the summer. The Earleys were telling me that the EU grant needs to be spent by that time. God help anyone having to work at this time of night. I hope they are getting good overtime.'

He pauses again and we stand for a quiet moment in the full moon over Kildare.

'You know most of the boys down there aren't from here,' he says.

'No,' I say.

'They are from all over the world. A few of our own but not many.'

'There will be the odd Donegal man down there, I am sure.'

He laughs. 'Yes, those Donegal ones love to build. You know that your uncle Jack and his sons worked on the Channel Tunnel?'

'I remember you telling me. What must that have been like?'

'I couldn't stand it but they love being down in the dirt digging. He is a very smart man, your uncle Jack. His boys too. Those ones could build you a tunnel to Australia if you gave them enough spades.'

'Are they still over in England?'

'All but Damian. He is in Australia now, working in the outback. Loves it apparently. Do you know that they fly him out to his site every month? Fly! He is so far out in the outback that it is the quickest way to get him there.'

'What must that be like?' I ask.

The moon stood still while the men in the distance scurried around. We could hear the sound of a digger reversing, the beep, beep, beep carrying across the far fields.

'That will be some motorway when it is finished,' he says, 'but isn't it odd how few of our own are working on it? They tell us that the EU grants will make us rich but our own are still leaving like they have always left. I thought there would be more in it for us.'

'They are calling them the New Irish,' I said.

'Well, if they are the New Irish, does that make us the New Woodkerns, stuck out here in the wilderness?'

'Don't say that out loud,' I cautioned, 'they will call you racist.'

'Oh, I know.'

In truth, it was the same in my office. The Americans wanted drones who spoke French, German, Italian and Spanish well. We only spoke English. They brought in beautiful Birgitte from Copenhagen and handsome Sven from Sweden and gorgeous Lucia from Italy. We were a minority in our own office.

'It is strange, alright,' I said.

We watched the workers for a little longer. The moon held steady and silver above us.

'I should go back,' he said.

'Let me sit with him tonight,' I said, 'you sleep.'

He hesitated. I could see the tiredness in his body. My father was slipping from middle age into old age. His hair had become a little thinner and a lot greyer.

'It is no problem,' I said, 'I will wake you if I need to.'

'Alright,' he said, his voice cracking.

We walked to the back door, pushed it gently aside.

'Do you want a cup of tea?' my father asked.

'No, I will be fine.'

'Alright. Well, thank you. Wake me up if, you know, if you need to.'

'Of course.'

My mother guided me into the bedroom where my grandfather lay. 'There is no change. The nurse was with him earlier. He seems comfortable. There are some Rosary beads on the bedside cabinet if you want them.'

'Thanks,' I said and sat beside my grandfather.

'Good night,' she said brusquely. She was not happy that I had not been down in such a long time. I tried to apologise but she brushed me aside. 'That man did everything for you. Worked himself to the bone raising your father and his family. He deserved more from you than the odd bottle of Jameson's.'

Grandfather did not stir. I had nothing more to do than to stay with him and watch over him until morning. I could hear my parents going to bed, the creak of the bathroom door, distant voices fading away as they finished their long day. My grandfather lay there, his shallow breathing filled the room. I lifted the beads out of boredom. What day was it? Which mystery? Glorious? Sorrowful? I could not remember the order. My mother was the one who had called out the decades when we were younger. I should have asked her before she left which mystery was meant for tonight. I should have paid more attention when I was younger. I resented the Rosary then, resented the few minutes to rattle out Hail Mary after Hail Mary. I always buried my head in the cushion, muttered what had to be muttered and then, finally, freed myself from the soft cushion to breath in the fresh air. My ungraciousness did not go unnoticed or unremarked on.

'Make more of an effort,' my mother had said, 'it is only a few minutes.'

I never made more of an effort.

The beads were made of wood and had been a gift to my mother from a priest who had been in the Holy Land. They glinted crimson in the lamp's light. I rubbed them between thumb and finger and a quiet 'Hail Mary' came unbidden. I stopped, knelt down, blessed myself and began again formally. An Our Father to begin with, then the Hail Marys. I moved the beads through thumb and finger. That's ten. Now a Glory be to the Father. I finished the five decades and began 'Hail Holy Queen, Mother of Mercy, hail thy life, thy sweetness and thy hope ...'

The prayer tumbled out of me, emerging from my darkest memory. I had not prayed it in years but it was still there, a prayer-poem that fell out of me when needed. I rose again and sat. My grandfather was still breathing. He had wasted badly over the last part of his sickness. This man who had spent his life in manual labour, as strong as an ox, was now reduced to a stick. Even after leaving the trains, he had carried on digging. He had built a little greenhouse for his tomatoes and potatoes. He was often to be found there, bent down, inspecting the shoots as they emerged from the grainy soil. He loved his potatoes; the tomatoes were for granny. They never peeled their potatoes but washed the dirt off them until the marbled skin appeared. They steamed them too, rather than boil them, and then, to eat, lots of butter and salt. He would sit there spearing potatoes with a fork in one hand and a glass of milk in the other. No emperor ever ate better.

Granny died before him, an unexpected fall and she was gone. He grieved her loss every day. He cried at her funeral Mass, cried as we lowered her into the ground, cried at her Month's Mind and every time her name was mentioned thereafter. He was bereft and we could do little to comfort him other than to sit with him, ask about the potatoes and tomatoes, help him buy the odd bag of compost, cook him his dinner. We watched him for years and this now was the final watching.

I had abandoned him years ago when I went to university. My trips home became less frequent, and then the job gave me an extra reason not to fulfil my duties.

'You should call and see your grandfather,' my mother said, 'he is always asking after you.'

'I will, I will. Next time when I have a bit more time to spare.'

This night had become next time. I had plotted and chased after Lucia and ignored all others. I had let work rule my life and had found financial reward. 'That's a lot of money to tell the time.'

My grandfather coughed. 'Grandfather. It's me. Are you ok?'

There was no reply. I reached for the water on the bedside cabinet and poured the smallest amount on his lips. The water dribbled down his chin and I dabbed at it with a tissue. His breathing was still so shallow, his chest rising ever so slowly and then, then, a final cough. I had to wake my father.

'What is this?' Tim had asked.

'Oh,' I said embarrassed, 'it's just peasant food. Something very simple.'

'Who taught you how to make it?' he asked.

'My mother. She was worried I would get scurvy when I was a student. She sat me down and showed me how to cook it. I have been cooking it for years. It's not fancy but I thought it would do for a half-time feed.'

The television had been muted. Ireland were losing.

'What do you call it?' asked Sven.

'Oh, it's just mince, carrots and potatoes. You soften the onion, brown the mince, add the stock and carrots. I just use stock cubes, one beef and one vegetable. If you use two beef it is too strong. Then steam the potatoes, put them in a bowl and pour the mince and carrots over the lot. Is it ok?'

'It is delicious,' said Tim.

'Yes, absolutely delicious,' added Sven, 'proper Irish cuisine.'

I laughed. 'Irish spaghetti more like. There's more if you want it. I always make a huge pot. You can put it in the fridge when it's cold and have it the following day. Tastes better to be truthful.'

They both raised their empty bowls as the referee returned to the pitch for the second half.

Sinéad has left. She could not stand the work anymore. 'You're mad,' I said, 'you will never get a better paid job than this.'

She looked at me with sadness. 'This work is shit; a total waste of time.'

It was not like her to swear.

'But the money? If you stay for ten years, you get shares.'

'I could not stick this for ten years.'

"What are you going to do?'

'I am going to teach in a Gaelscoil. I got on a course.'

'A Gaelscoil? Are you mad? Teaching Irish. That is a waste of time.'

'I would rather spend my life teaching Irish than localising shit.'

She lifted her cardboard box to her chest. 'Clara and a couple of the others are meeting me in the pub for a farewell drink. You are more than welcome to come.'

'I can't. I have to meet Lucia.'

'Isn't she still going out with Tim?'

'Yes, but he is back in Holland for the weekend and she wanted to go to the pictures. I could bring her after?'

'You should have more respect for yourself,' she said and left.

The funeral cortege was delayed by the road works even though we had left at first light. We had to skirt around the unfinished new motorway and use the old main road. We crawled along the small roads and stopped, briefly, at the station where grandfather finished his career. I could see people standing on the platform wondering what was going on. One of the workers came out. He stretched a hand into the window and shook my father's hand. Then we moved on, down more small narrow roads until we found the slip road to the completed part of the motorway. We paid the toll – 'nothing is ever free' – and then headed north to Donegal where he was to be buried. He had asked this of us, that we would return him to Donegal and that he be laid in the cemetery with his wife and his own kind.

I had been on this road many times before. We always holidayed in Donegal when I was younger. At the beginning it was the great adventure. I always wanted to travel with my grandfather and grandmother. They had the best sweets. My father and mother and my siblings would follow in the car behind. Later, as they got older, I had to travel with my parents. 'It is the fair thing to do,' my father said. I sulked.

The tension grew as we approached the Border. The fortifications looked down on us while the young soldiers moved from car to car, sometimes asking a question, looking for a driving licence and, other times, just waving us through. We all felt the tension lift as we finally crossed over at Newry, but it would return again at Strabane where even more menacing corrugated iron and soldiers waited for us. It was only once we crossed into Lifford and took the backroad to Letterkenny that we all felt safe.

'Do you know how many counties we passed through?' my father asked me once. I was still sulking. 'No.'

'Make a guess,' he said.

'Kildare, Meath, Tyrone, Donegal,' I said.

'Ach come on,' he said, 'try again. Aren't you studying geography for your Leaving Cert? Try again.'

'We started in Kildare, went through Meath, down the road to Newry ...'

'Go on; what county was in between?'

'Louth!' I said, 'Louth!'

He laughed.

'Then?'

'Armagh. Tyrone. Donegal. Six.' I said. 'That's six.'

He laughed, again. 'Almost. You have missed one.'

I thought again. 'I don't know. Are you sure?'

'Down. That little short cut we take in Newry goes through Down. You are travelling in seven of Ireland's thirty-two counties.'

No soldiers stopped us as we reached the Border this time. The fortifications were empty. We reached Newry and headed to Armagh and then into Tyrone and north towards Strabane and Lifford. The fort at Strabane stood silent and the only delay was caused by the volume of traffic on the road. The road from Lifford to Letterkenny was as bad as ever and we ground to a halt coming into Letterkenny itself. 'They are never finished building this place,' my father whispered in sadness. Finally, we found our road, drove up, past the hospital, crested the top of the town and drove down towards the distant rocky green hills. 'Some view,' said my father, 'it is some view.'

The road before us was empty. After a few miles we turned west and took the back road around Errigal. Here we had to drive at a snail's pace; the road was pitted with potholes and shaved away by grass verges. We passed under the mountain. When I was younger I was always frightened that it would topple down on top of me, but it never did. It was always there, unchanging, defiant.

The last time I had made this journey, my father had driven my grandfather. I had been enlisted, against my will, to accompany them North. I had no interest in making the journey, but my mother would not accept my excuse of work. Usually, grandfather drove but this time it was my father. They chatted occasionally on the road. When we finally made it to the family home, my grandfather gently touched my father's hand on the gear stick in thanks. 'Good man,' he said.

'Will I go in with you?' my father had asked him.

'Give me a couple of minutes to break the bad news and then follow me in,' he said.

'What bad news?' I had asked from the back seat. They did not answer.

We paused again at the foot of the mountain where my grandfather had been born and reared. There were cars lined along the road, pointing west to the chapel and the graveyard. Uncle Jack came towards us and bent down by the open window. They shook hands silently. He said to my father. 'They are all waiting at the chapel. We will follow you.' They shook hands again. My father managed a choked. 'Alright.'

We headed a little further on, left the mountain behind, found the main road again and travelled onto the chapel. The crowds had already gathered in their hundreds; the Gallaghers had come to bury one of their own. I saw uncles and cousins rise up from the walls around the chapel, ravens in black suits and ties. Cigarettes were tossed to the tarmac and ground underfoot. They came towards us, hands raised in recognition and sorrowful welcome. They would carry my grandfather the rest of the way. My father crumbled in his seat and cried violently for a moment. He caught his breath again, cleared his eyes and opened the door. 'Well lads,' he said.

Lucia kissed me in my office when we were alone. We had been chatting. I leant in and gently kissed her. She let me. I kissed her again and put my arms around her. She did the same. I raised my hand to her right breast. She drew it away. She was wearing a red jumper. I tried again. She drew my hand away again.

'Are you still going out with Tim?' I asked.

'I wish people would stop asking me that.'

Not a yes or a no. That was always her way. We kissed again. There was no passion on her part.

'Would you like to go out with me?'

She sighed. 'I don't want to be tied down.'

'But we kissed.'

'It is just a kiss.'

She danced with a newcomer from Norway that night in the pub in Dún Laoghaire: his arms wrapped tightly around her waist as they attempted a céilí dance. Later, she came back to us as we sat at our table, rubbing her nose. 'He hit me by accident when we were dancing.'

I looked away, sorry he hadn't broken it.

We buried grandfather in the graveyard by the sea. I helped lower his coffin down into the dark, sandy soil. The tears came then and fell down with his remains. The priest called for a last Hail Mary in Irish and I stepped away towards the cemetery wall to try and catch my breath. Many of the headstones were speckled in Irish, like Ogham on ancient monuments. The words cut in stone were a final public recognition to those whose language we did not speak, an admonishment to our failure. Here, however, in one last act of defiance against the State, Ó Domhnaill, Ó Docharthaigh, Mac Suibhne, Ó Gallchobhair, Ó Baoill, gave voice to their ancestors and to their history. Here were the remains of those who had survived famine and fire, who had fought with Aodh Ruadh, who had carved lives out of shore and sea, who had travelled across the water to Scotland and beyond to the New Island, to the world beyond the waves, to more poverty, more loneliness but who had survived, earned dollars and pounds, shillings and pence, and had sent it home in the hope that it would feed parents and siblings, that tomorrow would be a little easier, not just as hard, not just as unforgiving. *I ndilchuimhne,* I read again and again and again, in loving memory.

I rested on the solid stone and stared out to the island from where my grandfather's people had originally come. It had been abandoned in the 1950s but, now, in dribs and drabs, people had begun to return to their ancestral holdings during the summer. He had taken me there once, a lifetime ago, on a small boat whose little engine seemed incapable of travelling that far. Grandfather had instructed me where to sit and not to move about. There were no lifejackets for anyone, but he told me, if the boat were to tip over, that I was to hold on and not to try and swim to shore. I looked at him in fear. 'It won't tip over. It is just in case.' I knew I would be safe.

There was a gravestone by the wall to a British sailor who had died during the Second World War. 'A British Sailor: Known unto God.' What had happened to tip his boat and his life into the sea, the poor man? No one had come to claim him but I had heard the story of how his body had been found on the beach. The authorities in Dublin were contacted and they contacted London but no one could give his remains a name. His clothes were the only hint of who he had been and his role in life. The locals buried him in the end, placed him amongst their own and prayed over him on Cemetery Sunday.

'Donncha?'

I turned, it was Sinéad. I wiped the tears away. 'What has you here? Did you come all this way?'

She blushed. 'No. I heard about your grandfather from the ones on the course. I am here brushing up my Irish. I thought I would come and pay my respects. I am sure your father is heartbroken.'

'Of course, I had heard you are teaching in the Gaelscoil in Lisabile now. That's great. How's it going?'

'Well, there is a lot of work, translating resources into Irish and the like, but the work is great. I am wrecked everyday but it is good work. Satisfying, you know.'

'You are localising Irish,' I said.

She laughed. 'Yes, in a way. And you? You are still with the Yanks?'

'For the moment.'

'Oh?'

'There is nothing really there for me, I think.'

She looked out silently towards the island.

'Have you ever been in the island?' I asked.

'No. Not yet. There is talk of going later on the course, if the water is not too choppy. Have you been in?'

'Oh, yes, my grandfather's people were from there once. He took me in. It is very quiet. Not much to do.'

'The shame of it was that they abandoned it at all. But that's modern life, unfortunately. Our heartlands are being worn down to nothing.'

'You are building a new heartland with your Gaelscoil,' I laughed.

She smiled. 'It might all come to nothing but, you know, there has been no spoken Irish where we are in hundreds of years. We are starting again. Did you ever speak Irish with him, your grandfather?'

'Just for orals, at exam time. He only spoke Irish with his wife – and then just to make sure we didn't know what they were talking about. I had no real interest. What was Irish worth to us?'

She grew silent again. 'A lot of people think that way.' She sighed. 'Well, I should be getting back. We have a class this afternoon. I am sorry again for your loss.'

I walked with her to the cemetery gate, her red curls glowing in the summer sun.

'Well ...' she said.

'Would you not come for a cup of tea and a sandwich? They will all be talking Irish. You could translate for me or treat it as research?'

She paused and glanced at the ground. 'I don't know.'

I was beaten, I thought. It was what I deserved. We walked on quietly. There was a little dip in the path outside the cemetery where the soft soil had been worn away by the rain. I reached out and offered her my hand for balance. She took it and did not let go.

The road has been completed for a couple of years now, but they have still not taken down the signs. They leave them hanging there as once the English left the heads of the Irish on spikes at the city gates. It is a different kind of conquest, but a conquest nonetheless, I think. There is talk of more motorways west and south. I stand with my father and watch the lights rip up and down the motorway at night.

'The traffic never stops,' he says.

'Busiest road in the country,' I reply, 'when there are not any accidents.'

'That's right. Barely a day goes by without some idiot running into another on that road. People need their heads looking at. They think it is a race track.'

'It is like a moat around the city,' I say, 'and we are on the wrong side of it. We live outside the New Pale.'

'We might be grateful for that yet,' he says. 'Where are all these strangers coming from? The place is full of them.'

'All over the world,' I say.

'How?' he asks. 'What is here for them? We have a fellow driving a train for us from God knows where. He is a shifty bastard.'

'Don't say that out loud.'

'Oh, I know. I mean I know he has to eat. It's just ...'

'What?'

'It is not as if we don't know how to drive trains or buses ourselves. I mean, not so long ago, that would have been a good job, something anyone would have been happy to get. Delighted, in fact. Good hours, overtime, pension. Sure, what more could you have asked for? Now, we have to share it with these ones. There was precious little enough for us for long enough and now everyone and his mother has an Irish passport. Is this what we get for hanging on and paying our dues?'

'Don't say that out loud.'

'Oh, I know.'

'The rich don't care who the helots are?'

'Helots?' my father asks.

'Slaves the Spartans kept to do all the dirty work.'

'Helots,' he says, 'I will remember that.'

We listen to the traffic.

'That motorway is a curse. I told you years ago you don't get anything for free,' he says.

I know he is right, but I do not have the courage to admit it publicly. He stops again and then asks. 'How is Sinéad?'

'Expecting again,' I say shyly.

He laughs warmly. 'Another one! Does your mother know?'

'Yes. I just told her.'

'She is delighted, I am sure. Another one. That will be three. You have enough for a fullback line if it's another boy.'

'Or a fullforward line,' I joked.

He laughs. 'None of ours were ever fast enough to be amongst the forwards. Another one. Well, congratulations.'

Thanks, I say, and don't add that, if it is a boy, Sinéad will probably go again. She wants a daughter.

'How's work?' he asks.

'Going fine. I have lots of bits and pieces from the local schools and businesses. Nothing too hard, installing computers, checking the software works. Basic stuff. Turn on, turn off.'

'And you have a new van, I see.'

'I got it at Earley's, a nice secondhand Ford. Not too many miles on the clock. Nothing fancy but very reliable.'

My father smiled. 'That's the way.'

I am on the roads most days now, a New Woodkern, travelling the ways no one in the city knows about. I pass through little places where people still hang on. The post office and the Guards have left. There is only the National School, the chapel and the GAA club. I see handfuls of people going to early Mass, diligent in their defiance, teachers going into the trenches in the hope that some of their work will stick, coaches stitching teams together with the leftovers. We survive on our own. The ones in the city do not care if we stay or leave, whether we live or die. They will find someone else to turn their computers on, drive their trains and dig their ditches.

'Many is the one that got a good deal down from the Earleys,' my father says.

'And I'm helping Séamus out too.'

'Oh?'

'I help him run some of the tests on the car's computers. There's a lot of software in cars now.'

'I am sure he is grateful for the help, especially since the father died.'

'He is a good man, Séamus.'

'The Earleys were always decent people. He will make a grease monkey of you yet.' He pauses again. 'Well, you are making a go of the new business?'

'Yes, thank God. There is work now. God knows what the future holds, but between Sinéad's teaching salary and my bits and pieces we should be alright.'

'Do you miss the other place and the Yanks?'

'No, not at all. I miss the money.'

(Lucia, I think, Lucia. She has gone to Silicon Valley with Sullivan to make her fortune. She will skin the Yanks for every dollar they have).

He laughs again. 'Money is not everything, believe it or not.'

The lights on the motorway scar the night's darkness. We hear an engine, loud and angry, bark in the night. A car slices down the motorway. 'Good God, he's flying.'

Another set of lights explode into the darkness and tear after the first set. The siren sounds like a banshee in the darkness.

'It's the Guards,' I say.

'I hope they catch the bastard,' my father says.

We watch the lights mingle together and then fade away under the full moon. Finally, there is peace.

We have decided to take down grandfather's greenhouse; it is full of broken glass. The dog chased a feral cat into it one day and the cat, in its panic, ran through the glass to escape. One broken pane led to another. It is beyond repair now. His little patch of land beside the greenhouse has also gone wild through our neglect. There will be no more homegrown potatoes. The drills he carefully dug are still just visible, but are now spotted with buttercups and clover. His spade stands lonely by the wall. A gardener's cross.

II

Ingeborg Bachmann

STERNE IM MÄRZ

Noch ist die Aussaat weit. Auf treten
Vorfelder im Regen und Sterne im März.
In die Formel unfruchtbarer Gedanken
fügt das Universum nach dem Beispiel
des Lichts, das nicht an den Schnee rührt.

MARCH STARS

Still it's too early for sowing. Fields
surface in rain, March stars appear.
Like an afterthought, the universe submits
to familiar equations, such as the light
that falls but leaves the snow untouched.

Translation by Peter Filkins

Elizabeth Éilís

Her name was Elizabeth, and her hair was as red as mine was black. We used to joke about that. She used to say, 'I am the true Gael and you are nothing but a Cruthin.' I would reply, 'Your ancestors probably raped some poor little wee girl when they came over with Chichester. That's why you are red, you bloody Planter.'

'Ha, you are just jealous because we have good land while you swamp dwellers have to make do with bog and stones.'

'And who drove us to the bogs? Who made us eat the stones? The dirty Planters. That's who.'

Elizabeth would stand and look at me in mock sadness, push her chest out like Maureen O'Hara in *The Quiet Man* and say in her poshest faux English accent, 'I say, you oik, we let you live, didn't we?'

And I would stand up like John Wayne and say, 'The hell you did. We just didn't let youse kill us all.' And that was that. That was the punch line. We would laugh. We played the scene out, kissed and folded into one another again, leaving history behind and enjoying the heat of the present.

We met at university in the city. I was one of the few Catholics studying German. When they called out our names, it sounded like a roll call for the police. There was one Fionnuala, one Fergal and myself, Alastair Pádraig Mulholland. The name echoed around the room like a shot in the silence. 'That's an unusual spelling of the name, Alastair and Pádraig,' the professor said.

'Yes,' I croaked from the back of the room, 'it's the Irish spelling.'

The lecturers, blue noses all, cast furtive glances, or did I imagine that? I could feel the mark of Cain on me. Alastair! I was the wild man who had landed in their midst, the dark threat of the other. The other Catholics didn't count: Fionnuala was a nice girl whose father was a doctor, and Fergal was from the Malone Road. He was soon adopted by the nice Protestant girls as their own little Fenian doll. He loved the attention and did his best to ignore me.

I did my best to talk to them; it was how I was raised. I was polite, swore as little as possible, tried to make small talk, complained about the reading we were expected to do and avoided politics, religion and Gaelic football entirely. Not that we could avoid politics; as the 1970s tipped into the 1980s and bodies still salted the streets. No, we were all marked by events over which we had no control. We were all put in our little cages and, truth be told, we did little to fight the stereotyping. It suited us all, at that moment, to nod politely and ignore the blood.

But Elizabeth, Elizabeth actually spoke to me. She did not go out of her way; it was not a case of 'some of my best friends are Catholics'. No, she just spoke to me. I had a copy of Heinrich Böll's *Where were you, Adam?* in my hand. She looked at me. 'That's cheating.'

'What?' I said and immediately corrected myself, saying 'Pardon?'

She looked like the kind of woman who expected 'pardon'.

'That's cheating,' she repeated, 'we are supposed to be reading that in German. Not in English.'

I caught the lightness of the mockery in her voice, just about. She was gently slagging me off. I knew this game from school.

'I mean, if you want to read it in English, go join the English Department.'

I knew she wanted a reply, but I could not find a witty one. 'Oh. I am reading it in English first to get the gist. Then I will read it in German for, you know, the, em, nuances.'

She smiled. 'I'm only joking. Can I borrow it after you? It will take me forever to read it in German.'

I reached the book across to her. 'Please, take it now. I have finished. Honestly.'

She took it in her polished nails, bright shiny shells, and smiled again. 'Thanks. I will give it back to you tomorrow.'

'There's no rush.'

'No. I will have it read by tomorrow.'

The tutor arrived and we filed into the room. I ended up sitting beside Fergal. He nodded but I ignored him. Elizabeth sat at the end of the table. The autumn sunlight shone through the skylight and lit up her red hair. I remember that still. I remember thinking just how red her hair was.

She was as good as her word and returned the book as promised the following day. We met by the Students' Union and I expected nothing more than a polite handover and to be on my way.

'Do you fancy a coffee?'

'Me?'

'Ja, du.'

(She had used the familiar form. Was that significant?)

I laughed. 'I can just about understand that.'

She did not want to go into the union. 'I know a better place.' I took the book, threw it into my satchel and followed her. She was beautiful. I felt like Oisín following Niamh Chinn Óir to the Land of Youth. She had found a little café where they served proper coffee. I remember her saying 'proper' and wondering what she meant. The café was bohemian but clean. (Elizabeth was never one for dirt). The coffee machine sat in the corner, belching steam, and the chalk board on the wall offered various Greek dishes I could not pronounce and had never eaten.

'I will have a double espresso,' said Elizabeth. 'What about you, Alastair?' She said *Alastair* in such a melodic way that I felt like a character in an opera. *Alastair,* she said, the syllables rolling out of her mouth. *Alastair. Don Alastair. Signor Alastair.*

'Oh, the same, I suppose,' not really knowing what I was ordering. 'Yes, I'll have the same. That sounds dead on.'

'Are you sure?' she said, 'it is quite strong?'

'No, no. I am sure it will be fine. That's why we are at university, isn't it, to try new things?'

I thought the waiter had made a mistake when the coffee came in thimbles.

She smiled. 'Not what you were expecting?'

'Maybe not,' I admitted, 'I usually just drink tea.'

I could smell the hot liquid rising from below, dark as treacle. 'Hot bog water,' I thought and drank. My tongue numbed up under the taste. Elizabeth laughed. I laughed. We laughed.

I reached for my wallet – it was the least Don Alastair could do. 'My shout,' I said but she paid before I had even got a note out. 'No,' she said, 'my treat for the loan of the book. I would not want you going back to the bog and telling them the Planters don't pay their way.'

'What? I mean. Pardon?'

'I don't want you bad mouthing the Prods back home. We get a bad enough press as it is. Just because we came over here four hundred years ago and stole your land.'

She blew into her coffee. The liquid rippled like the lough's surface in summer. Had I been indiscreet and said something I shouldn't? No. I was sure I had not, but she looked serious. She studied the coffee and then looked up and smiled. 'You should see your face.'

And we laughed. Again. We laughed. Again.

Elizabeth was the first woman I ever saw naked. Not entirely naked but near enough. We had gone for a swim in the pool. I was never a good swimmer but I knew that I wanted to see her in her swimsuit. I was hoping she would wear a bikini. She had a good figure. I could tell that much from her jeans and tops. She did not wear a bikini that day but a one-piece swimsuit. I was disappointed but it confirmed what I had already thought – she had a great figure. She dived in but I used the ladder. By the time, I turned around, she was already cutting her way down the pool. She could swim well; that much was obvious. She swam freestyle and her technique was perfect. I counted the strokes and watched as she turned her head to one side, breathed and then sank her lips beneath the water again. I could see her legs and the curve of her behind flash from the water as she pulled away. I splashed after her and did my best to keep pace. By the end of a few lengths, I could feel my muscles tighten and had to rest in the shallow end. She stopped briefly. 'Are you alright?'

'Oh, fine,' I said, 'just a bit sore. Football is more my thing.'

She stood up and stretched her arms behind her shoulders. Her suit had become sheer in the water and I could see her nipples, like two dark pebbles on a wet beach and an orange smudge on her lower body. I felt myself begin to rise and lowered my body deeper into the water to hide it. 'I will do a couple more lengths and then we will go,' Elizabeth said. I tried not to stir. She smiled. 'You had better rest. Don't expect me to give you the kiss of life if you get into trouble.'

She kicked off the wall and left; smiling, knowing.

I saw her naked again, later; much later. We were on our year abroad in Germany. She had been sent to Cologne and I had been sent to Koblenz. That year abroad was the making of me. That was the year I realised that I was not a fraud, that I had the necessary cunning to survive away from home. That was the year I discovered freedom, the year I realised that, whatever else happened, I never wanted to live at home. Germany and German were my future; this was my life raft to take me away from Ireland.

We met regularly that year. There was an ease to our friendship outside of the North. We were strangers in a strange land but more common to each other than had been the case at home but never free from home. I passed some graffiti one night with Elizabeth. RAF was scrawled on the wall. I had not been paying attention. 'RAF? Do you see that? There are your fly boys desecrating the place. No one here wants to be reminded of what the RAF did here during the war.'

For the first time, Elizabeth became angry. 'It means Red Army Faction. The Germans have terrorists too.'

Terrorists, a word Elizabeth had never used in front of me before. Terrorists. She moved on a little ahead of me and pretended to browse in the shops. Then she turned, beckoned and took my hand.

Her boyfriend – a George something – was away and after one glass too many of sweet German wine, she forgot him for a night. Till the day I die I will remember the sight of her raising her blouse over her head and seeing her fully naked. I rolled away from her later, another first for me along a road she had already travelled. I can still remember my breath catching in my chest, my open-mouthed gasps upwards. She smiled. 'Don't get used to that. Next time, I get to be on top.'

'Bloody Prods. You always want to be on top.'

'Yes, that's it. We like to keep you Taigs in your place.'

'Anyway, it's nice to see that those rumours about promiscuous Prods are actually true.'

She laughed. 'My poor, guilty, frustrated Fenian.' She stretched her limbs across me once more and I surrendered inch by inch while Van Morrison's *Astral Weeks* played in the background.

There were books; so many books. Elizabeth read like no one I have ever known. Her book shelves were full of works that I had never seen. The course work seemed so familiar to her. When I discovered Goethe, Storm, Rilke, Dürrenmatt, von Horvath for the first time, she had already moved on to ever more exotic work. She spoke of German poets I had never heard of and seemed to find the most modern and esoteric writers in little magazines and collections. I struggled to keep up. 'How can you have read so much?' I asked.

'Oh, I'm a couple of years older than you,' she said casually.

'What do mean? How many years?'

'I started university in England a couple of years ago but had to come home.'

'How many years? Why did you have to come home?'

'Oh,' she paused, 'a death, an unexpected death.' She paused. 'And as for my age ...' She looked at me, laughed, spoke and moved on. 'I am still more than able to keep up with you.'

They shot him as he left for work. He had been looking for his car keys in his briefcase when a gunman shot him repeatedly. The news said he was a solicitor, married with two children. The attackers had fled on a motorbike and the police were looking for *zeugen*. I struggled with the translation in my head. Witnesses, I thought, it must be witnesses in this context.

I recognised the street where the shooting had happened. It was not far from the school where I was teaching for the year. The reporter was talking quickly, panicked by the unfamiliar scene. He spoke of terrorism, that word I knew intimately. The pictures showed a body covered in a blanket; police and ambulance personnel milling about. It was senseless, I thought; what could they possibly hope to achieve by killing this poor man? Did they honestly think that the state would collapse over this corpse?

Should I mention this to the students? This happened all the time at home. I decided not to. I wanted to talk to them about the lough and fishing for eels. I always avoided politics and made only one small concession to the subject: the head had introduced me to them as being from 'Nord Irland'. I had nodded, smiled and, when he left, I said very slowly, in my most formal German. *'Ich heiße Alastair und ich stamme aus Irland.'*

My name is Alastair and I come from Ireland.

That was my blow against partition, my only blow.

I saw Elizabeth a couple of days after the killing and mentioned it to her. She turned away.

I owe Elizabeth my academic and literary career. It was she who gave me the little collection of poems with which I first made my name. Elizabeth undoubtedly had a wider knowledge of German literature than me, but I could see the possibilities better than her. I saw connections where she did not. It did not require a great leap to link the common themes of post-war German writing with the North's own poets. I got my Ph.D. on the back of that. I spent years deep in one of the rooms of the department reading everything I could. Yes, there may well have been a certain amount of bullshit in what I wrote then, but it was well-written bullshit and that really is all that literary criticism amounts to. So, I wrote about Heaney, Montague and Carson and threw them into the company of German writers. I took the themes of the Irish countryside, contentious history, language and killing, and sent them down the Rhine on my own little tourist boat of a thesis. The work caught the eye of a German publisher and, more amazingly again, the eye of the German literati. I found myself, still in my twenties – though just about – feted in German literary circles. The Irish were mysterious enough to the Germans back then; they thought we were spiritual, if fractious, Christians. The book and my academic qualifications led to a junior position in a German university. I had found my lifeboat. I jumped in and sailed it as far away from the lough shore as I could.

Elizabeth wanted to go to a céilí. I had had enough of them during my summer days in the Donegal Gaeltacht, but she wanted to go. We attached ourselves to a crowd from the Cumann Gaelach and found ourselves in a little club in the city one Saturday night. My Irish was poor, but good enough to pass in Cumann Gaelach circles.

'Aren't you nervous?' I asked her as the black taxi choked its way up the road.

"No,' she said. 'I have you.'

I kissed her then, in front of everyone, but she moved her head. 'I'll have to call you Éilís here,' I said. She laughed and said softly. 'Elizabeth Éilís.' We danced together all night. She had no fear and I soon realised that she was not altogether ignorant of what she was doing. 'Highland dancing,' she said and whirled away from me to the thump of a badly-played bodhrán. I never thought to ask where she had learned highland dancing.

'Is she yours?' he asked.

'What?' I turned. It was Mackle, the local student republican agitator.

'Is she yours?' he asked again.

'Yes, she is with me,' I said and knew, just knew, that the wee bollix was trying to sniff out her religion.

'She is not from around here?' he said.

'No, not everyone lives on the road.'

'Where is she from?'

'She's a culchie, like me.'

He drank again from his pint; his eyes were those of a travelling rat. His Irish was harsh and coarse. I could hear the lack of fluency and bad pronunciation even over the sound of the music. 'She's not from here though?' and he left to get another drink. I watched him leave and then turned; Elizabeth was in front of me again, looking towards Mackle and the bar. She put her arms around me, laid her head on my cheek and whispered 'It's time to go.'

She put her hand in mine and we left. We walked the maze of narrow streets while the windows shone with lights. A dog barked, another replied. We passed the chapel and found ourselves on the road again. Two armoured jeeps drove past, the smoke from their exhausts leaving a stinking grey trial in their wake. She put her arms around me as we waited for a taxi. 'I love you,' I said. She kissed me on the cheek and said nothing.

The best day we ever spent together was on the lough. My uncle had lent me his little boat and we set sail from the Moorland and headed into the lough. I talked to her about eels, fishing and ghost stories. She sat beneath the sail, taking it all in. I pointed out local landmarks, talked ninety to the dozen and then just stopped. She smiled, lay back, and we just listened to the breeze in the sail. She turned to me then.

'Can we stop for a moment?'

'Are you feeling sick?'

'No,' she said. 'I just want to swim.'

'I didn't bring any trunks.'

'You don't need trunks.'

I dropped anchor; she stood up, stripped off her clothes and dived in. I panicked for a moment as she disappeared into the lough. Then she came up, her red hair like seaweed.

'Are you mad?' I shouted, 'the water will be freezing.'

'Get them off, big boy,' she shouted.

I went in after her. It was the first time I had swum naked in the lough. The water was freezing, but she did not seem to feel the cold. I saw her disappear under water, once, twice. I splashed about until finally she said 'That's enough.' She pulled herself onto the boat easily, her naked skin dripping silver in the sunshine.

The parting was due to work. I got a job in Germany and fled. I did not want to die for Ireland, or talk shite for Ireland, or protest for Ireland. I wanted to live. I wanted wine, women and song. I wanted long naked walks along German beaches; sunny days on the Rhine; pot in Berlin. I did not want to be a victim; I did not have to be a victim. I could get out and make something of myself, and I did. I got a university position and left without as much as a glance back.

I wrote to Elizabeth in the old-fashioned way with pen and paper, asked her to come out after me, asked her to keep in touch, asked her to live with me. She did not follow me. She wrote, told me she was working at home, but did not say doing what. Said she was enjoying her new job and would keep in touch and, who knows, perhaps something more might have come of it; but there were other women, other beautiful German women. Bit by bit, I began to ignore Elizabeth's letters.

The success went to my head. I stopped writing to everyone, stopped phoning everyone, stopped talking to everyone. I did nothing but study and lecture, and ended up writing another book that made my name, a collection of essays on Europe and culture that just caught the mood of the times perfectly – Zeitgeist, baby, Zeitgeist. I was a writer, a critic, a cultural guru, someone worth listening to. I was feted and took up every opportunity I could to travel, bedded every willing woman who crossed my path, gave up on the glory of God and the honour of Ireland and counted the money and naked flesh as it rolled in.

I meant to write to Elizabeth again, but laziness and indifference held me back. Then, there she was, a picture of her on the German news, her beautiful red hair framing those green eyes, the words RUC, dead, bomb, civilians, pouring out of the television. I saw pictures of tarpaulins stretched over bodies. She was lying there, ripped asunder before me. I thought of her naked in my bed, thought of her reading with me, walking with me, talking with me, her hand in my hand, her beautiful red hair. Her last postcard was on the shelf. 'Are you ok? I have not heard from you in months.'

They declared a ceasefire and, a little while after that I saw Mackle on the steps of Stormont as culture minister, still speaking very bad Irish.

I tried to find her grave one bitter March. I had had to come home; Inga had thrown me out when she found me with another woman. I could not help myself; she was young and beautiful and my wedding ring meant nothing to her. I still had some cachet as a writer, some dim shine of past fame. I would have preferred not to have been caught, but still hoped to manage the problem. My parents were suspicious, but they knew by this stage that I lacked their discipline in religion and life. I had surrendered long ago to my impulses; I could deny myself no pleasure if offered.

They confronted me but I laughed them off. 'I am an Augustinian kind of Catholic. You know, save me, Lord, but not yet.' Their faces soured with my sarcasm. I did not care. Bit by bit I had cast off any pretence at religious observance. I no longer kept Lent; did not go to Mass on Easter or at Christmas, and worshipped all things material. My suits were from Hugo Boss; I collected expensive Pelican fountain pens; I drove a Porsche, travelled to any event that was paid for, ate well, drank better. I wanted to be modern, and being modern meant not being an Irish Catholic. I mixed with people who mocked my faith and I joined in. I did not care. I cared only for recognition and advancement. Yet, strangely, the further I travelled from what I disdained the less original my thought had become. My peers had thought me more spiritual than them because I came from a Christian land and a devout people. Gradually, they realised that I was as venal as them, worse indeed. I was not the Irish writer of their imagination, but the cute, cunning whore they had not known existed on the island.

Cutting myself off from my roots meant that my imagination had begun to calcify bit by bit. The well became overgrown with weeds. I had no new insights because I had no belief in anything. I realised too late that the most original thing about me in the modern world was the fact that I had been raised an Irish Catholic on a small, ancient island on the edge of Europe. I was now no better than the old Gael who bent the knee to English royalty.

The insight came too late. I could not write anything of value to save myself. The publishers and critics knew it. They said nothing publicly; no one ever does, just in case the miraculous happens and the faded becomes famous once again and needs to be courted.

Worse, the peace process had removed our bloody moods from the continental media; larger concerns loomed in the East and in the Mediterranean. I could not find my footing in this new world.

In desperation, I had pitched a translation project to a number of my former publishers. None had been interested. A smaller publisher agreed in the end, but my happiness faded quickly; I could not find myself in the work. I could not work. I had become soft; my star had faded.

It was a poem by Montague that made me think of her again:

> Again your lost, hurt voice:
> I hope this never happens to you,
> I wouldn't wish it upon anyone:
> To live and dance in lonely fire,
> To like awake at night, listening
> For a step that cannot come.

She was before me again, living, dancing, a step that could not come. She was in the pool before me, in the pub in Koblenz, in my bed, reading at my side, writing her final postcard to me, lying on a road bleeding to death. I did not care. I had gotten away. I had done no harm. It was not my fault. I cried then, thinking about her and threw myself out the door towards the car. 'I have a message to run,' I shouted at my parents as they returned from Mass, 'I will be back later.'

I knew she had lived on the other side of the lough. I threw the car down the back roads and headed across the boggy lanes, splashed white by spots of late snow. This was Catholic land, bad land. Here was the chapel and the

GAA club; here were the poor, hungry fields for the survivors of past wars, the unwanted acres of bog, water and weeds. Here the intimate language of people and place was set aside while we carried on blessing ourselves in English. That, in itself was still enough to mark us different. Here the roads, known only to locals, disintegrated year by year. Foreign concrete and native soil wrestled day by day to see who would be champion.

I still remembered the hidden paths from my younger days; they had not improved. The rushes stood by the roadsides, chewing back at the black treacle tarmac. The Porsche moved like a slug, the wheels spinning in protest against Irish stones, longing for smooth German motorway.

I passed the lonely cross to a Catholic man murdered by loyalists, withered flowers marked his end. They had been scattered by the wind and the rain but some petals still shone brightly on the ground, little shards of yellow and red that pinned his sacred memory to the bloody sheugh. Ash and willow trees, shorn by the cold, stood as vigilant guards over his ghost. They shaded him from view in the summer and, in winter, the leaves cast themselves aside to remind passersby of the human sacrifice. I said an unbidden prayer; remembered his name, his smiling face from the newspaper and turned left.

(That German solicitor from Koblenz, I thought, what was his name? What was *his* name?)

In a tree a buzzard sat sullen, his wings wrapped around him like the mantle on an ancient Irish chieftain. There was no thermal today to carry him to the heavens. The car engine startled him and he rose reluctantly from his viewing post to let out a shriek in anger against the disturbance. His wings spread wide, and I could see his dappled feathers stretching in the gloom.

Then came the good land, the Planters' land, large fields, the Orange Hall and the grey brick buildings that marked the Protestant regiments of Church of Ireland and Presbyterian jostling for souls. She had lived here, somewhere here. She was buried here, somewhere here. I remembered the name of her village, found it with clean cars strung out along the roadside for Sunday services. I should stop. I should ask. They would understand. They would have known her. They would not have forgotten her. I should stop and wait. Someone would know her and point me in the right direction.

I did not stop. I could not stop. I carried on, leaving Anglican, Evangelical, Presbyterian and Methodist behind. It was too late; it was just too late. I saw the sign for Londonderry. It had not been reimagined, as it had been in my own locale, to 'Derry'. The road was suddenly firm. I followed the sign and the car roared in thanks for the good tarmac. My speed rose. I would not go back. The car shot forward even faster. I would not go back. I would go west, to the edge of Ireland, to the cliffs.

I would just go and let the lonely fire burn me to the bone for once and for all.

III

Happy are those
who do not follow the advice of the wicked,
or take the path that sinners tread,
or sit in the seat of scoffers;
but their delight is in the law of the LORD,
and on his law they meditate day and night.

– Psalms 1.2

Father Monsignor

He woke slowly, then suddenly. The sacristy was empty. He glanced at his watch. No, he hadn't missed the wedding. There were still about forty minutes before Mass. He had dozed off without realising it. His breviary lay in his hands, still open. He closed it and blinked. He was alone. No matter. He was used to that by now and had learnt not to dwell on his loneliness. Self pity, he had come to realise, was of no use. Better by far to think on the good things, on the gifts that every day brought.

He remembered thanking the sacristan for his help in preparing the altar. 'No problem, Monsignor,' the sacristan said. 'Not long to go now for you.'

'No, Harry, not long. This Mass and one more.'

'Aye. And you're coming along after to the hall for a cup of tea. We'd hate for you to leave without a cup of tea.'

'Oh, yes, Harry. I'll be there. I'm looking forward to that,' said the Monsignor. He recognised it as a lie in his heart as soon as he spoke it. He was not looking forward to it, not one bit. If he could leave the city immediately after the Mass he would have done so. He had thought about coming up with some excuse to run out of the chapel as soon as the Mass ended, to head north towards the coast and home. He hadn't the heart, though, to do it. It would have been too cruel, and he wasn't cruel. He knew there would be parishioners who would miss him, and he would miss one or two of them as well. But he had spent a lifetime as a priest and had grown a little hard in his dealings with parishioners – often shadowboxing with them, allowing them the sense of being close and friendly to him, but always hanging back a little from them. In his early days as a priest he thought of himself solely as their shepherd, someone who needed to guide his flock. He recognised his own arrogance now with shame. He had been well-educated at school and in the seminary after. He had read Aquinas in Latin, and Plato in Greek, and came to his ministry full of abstract thought and high purpose. He had hoped that the Bishop might send him to Rome so that he might carry on his studies. The Bishop had other ideas. 'We have no need of intellectuals. Knuckle down in your parish and you will be fine. God bless now.'

He had kissed the Bishop's ring, withdrew without protest and let parish life whittle his pretentions away gradually. The Bishop – God rest his soul – had decided to send him to the city, and it was in the city that he had spent the greater part of his ministry. He had not understood why the Bishop could not have given him a rural parish closer to his parents, but accepted the Bishop's direction with humility and found himself tracing the city's borders as a young curate. The accent grated with him then and now. It held none of the sweetness of his native North Antrim speech. The nasal, whiny way in which so many city people spoke irked him, and it was a source of no little pride that, after almost fifty years exile in concrete, he had not lost the soft sounds of his townland. He felt pride when new acquaintances remarked that he was from North Antrim. 'Born and bred,' the Monsignor would say. 'Born and bred.'

'Have you been in the city long, Father?'

'A lifetime.'

'And you have never picked up the accent?'

'Nah,' he would say if feeling mischievous and sometimes, just sometimes, the other person would get the joke.

A lifetime. Yes, a lifetime in the service of God. He could feel the weight on his shoulders almost. He could sense his own impatience to complete this Mass and be away. He bent his head and drove down into his own being. 'No,' he said, 'be patient. Deliver this Mass as if your life depended on it.' The word 'sacrament' rolled around his head and he could feel himself becoming calm. 'Sacrament,' he said aloud. The word anchored him. He said it again, 'sacrament', and found peace.

He had spent a lifetime delivering the sacraments. He was a priest. He could be nothing but a priest. He had a vocation. He had always had a vocation. He recognised God's will early in his life. His parents had been unsure but were reluctant to deter him. His father asked only that he go to college first and qualify as a teacher before going into the seminary. He did as his father asked, but still found himself drawn towards the priesthood. There was no pressure and he was not needed at home; the farm was too small to share and would be Séamus's inheritance as first-born. He, however, would have to make his way in the world and, he reasoned, the priesthood was to be his path. Oddly, he had felt no fear in leaving for Maynooth, no sense of doubt, but rather one of belonging and fulfilment. The regime was no better or worse than what he had been used to at school. He went where he was told to go and did what he was told to do. The rules and regulations caused him no difficulty. No, he thought, that was not entirely true. He missed the hurling. He missed the camaraderie of team and playing; he missed the swing of the stick and the soft, soft contact of bos and sliotar. He missed the sound as the ball flew away, bent through the heavens by the will of his hurl. He missed the sight of sliotar skimming through the posts or, even better, the way in which it was smothered in the net for a goal, and then, the roar, the dark deep roar of his teammates. 'Good man! Good man!'

In many ways he had missed that more than the women. He had had to forego the game entirely but was often in the company of nuns and mothers and wives. They, oddly, had remained a constant in his life while the glory of his hurling days had faded ever further away. His one surrender to sentiment was to have always kept a hurley wherever he went. The sacristan had found it funny to find one with the rest of his luggage when he came to his final parish.

'Are you expecting trouble, Father? We are not as bad as people make us out, you know.'

'No, not at all. I know. It's a little something from home.'

'You're from Clonedun, Father, isn't that right?'

'No, I'm from Clonedall.'

'Isn't it the same, Father?' asked the sacristan.

'No, it isn't,' he replied. He amazed himself that he still found the mix-up to be annoying after all these years. Clonedall was his home; he was a 'Dall man and still found people's sour ignorance grating. Oh, the city ones loved to hold forth about their own wee streets. They would offer you virtual tours of areas long since lost to redevelopment, but they could not, would not, did not care to distinguish between Clonedun and Clonedall. But mix up someone from the Turf Field with someone from the Bright Rock and they would bristle. 'No, I'm from the other side of the road.'

He knew why – his geography was simply not important to them. That was one of the things that had most surprised him when he first came to the city; their sense of being at the centre of the universe. At first he thought they were just joking, but he came to realise they were not. The city was their world. There was nothing of worth outside the city to them. They would holiday in Donegal and return like thankful wartime refugees who had finally been allowed home by a conquering power.

'It's great to be home,' they would say, 'it's great to be back.'

He would look at their pinched, little houses and their narrow streets and wonder how they found any beauty in them at all. His nose wrinkled when he thought of some of the slums he had served in as a curate. He had seen hungry children walk barefoot to school in order to keep their shoes good. He had been in schools where a single class had sixty pupils in the one room. He had known doctors who had spoken of malnutrition and childhood diseases that belonged in another age. He had seen large families raised in houses little bigger than shoeboxes and fed on wages little better than a serf's. But raised they were and fed they were and educated they were. That was what he found most surprising of all – that bullish refusal to surrender. He laughed aloud. 'No surrender,' he said, 'no surrender.'

They had not surrendered, he thought. They had needed that stubbornness from partition and throughout the Troubles. He remembered the early days when the violence first broke out, the sense that something uncontrollable had been unleashed. He had still been a relatively young man then but could not fathom the violence that people his age and younger had in them. He had watched the riots being organised. He watched the older ones hang back and signal to the younger ones to begin. A flick of the finger was all that was needed and the jackals were let loose. He saw a mob storm a bus, their screams rising in the air. 'Get off the fucking bus! Get off the fucking bus! Now! Everyone off the fucking bus!'

Young men, armed with little more than their fists, screamed at the driver. He needed no second invitation.

He raised his hands in the air and moved to leave. The passengers left after them, the young ones running in fear, the older ones in anger that their journey home had been interrupted, but too scared, nonetheless, to confront the masked rioters. He remembered the old lady, weighed down with shopping bags, who was the last to leave. The ringleader was still shouting. 'Get off the fucking bus!' She, flustered but still dignified, was no soft touch. She rounded on the rioter with fearless contempt. 'You're a fucking disgrace, ye wee bastard, a fucking disgrace! I have to carry these bags all the way up the road now. You're the one who should fuck off, you and your whole fucking family!'

The ringleader faltered, not expecting such violent language. The old lady carried on. 'You're a fucking disgrace! A fucking disgrace, the lot of youse.' She gathered her bags around her, divided them into two equal piles and began to lift them. One of the other passengers, a young woman, approached her. 'Here, I'm going up the road. I can give you a hand.'

'Ah, God bless you, love. You're a dote. Thank you so much.'

They heaved the bags up. The old lady turned towards the rioters one last time. 'Youse are a fucking disgrace! Away off and wreck your own homes!' She walked on up the road, her dignity intact. The rioters laughed at their leader. He hesitated, wondering whether he should go after the old lady. He decided not to. 'Right, let's move this across the road.'

The other drivers on the road knew what was coming. Those who could made a dash to get past the bus before it was too late. The drivers of the bread van and the milk lorry cut deep turns into the tarmac and headed in the opposite direction. They had no desire to let the rioters burn their trucks and lose their livelihood.

One of the rioters jumped in the bus's cab and started it. The engine coughed and the bus jumped a foot or two before stalling. He tried again and it stalled again. The leader shouted 'I thought you could fucking drive?'

'A car. I can drive a fucking car. I can't get the hang of the clutch on this. It keeps stalling,' the second rioter cried out.

'Fuck it,' said the ringleader, 'We'll just light her up where she is. No one will get past it anyway.'

They threw bricks through the windows and then petrol bombs. It took a while before the flames caught hold but once they did the black incense rose to the heavens. There was no way past now.

The ring leader looked across the road to the real leader, leaning against the wall of a local supermarket. He gave another swish of his finger and the jackals dispersed. He had recognised the real leader, a sly one, he thought. He will keep his hands clean and let others do the dirty work.

They had all to tiptoe around the bus for weeks to come until, finally, it was scrapped off the road. The burnt tarmac and broken glass lingered longer, however, while the British army helicopter hovered in the sky above.

Things got worse. He was called out once for a man who had been shot dead by the British army. The body lay crumpled on the road in a lough of sticky blood. The RUC man nodded to him. 'He's over there, Father.' The soldiers opened up a passage to let him through.

'What happened?' he asked the policeman.

The policeman hesitated and then whispered, 'Your man tried to blow them up but they caught him at it. He made a run for it but, well, they weren't going to let him get away with it.'

He knelt trembling before the broken body. The man's jeans had fallen around his waist while his shirt had risen up towards his shoulders. The sudden violent impact of the bullets had disrobed and disembowelled him in one go; his flesh parted as the bullets spun through his body. The wounds were clearly visible, a deep gash that cut from his back to his front which let white, shattered bone shine from his chest. The priest felt his own heart stop, closed his eyes and began his prayers. He thought of the man's family and what was to come. He thought of what the man had wanted to do to the soldiers. A bomb! On this street. It did not bear thinking about. Who had sent him, this child? He thought again of the rioters. Was he one of them? The prayers fell faltering from his lips. He felt the policeman behind him. 'Are you done, Father?'

He nodded. 'Done for now.'

There were other broken bodies, people who left their house and did not return: children killed at school and shop; the grandmother blown up in a bomb; the married couple shot as alleged informants. And then the justification, the denials, the lies, the evil words used to cover the corpses. 'One of those things.' 'They deserved it.' 'Regrettable.'

His soul sank. So much blood spilt until some kind of sense grew. Talks about talks began, then talks, then more talks and then, finally, a ceasefire of sorts. He saw them in their cavalcade, waving their tricolours out the window, claiming victory, driving past the burnt-out buses and long-forgotten corpses, pretending it had been worth it, pretending they had won. All the while the British army helicopter still hovered in the sky, watching.

He could still not make sense of it, of the raw rage that had gripped so many people for so long. The city he first knew in the 1950s bore little resemblance to the shape and mood of the city as the millennium approached. The green fields of his days as a young curate had long been concreted over with houses, and the fistful of parishes he first knew had been surrounded by newer ones, so much so that they stretched from the city centre out into what had been the countryside. The church had spread far and wide throughout the city, setting up new parishes, trying to keep pace with the people, and trying to instil a sense of God in them.

He remembered his first mass in the city, down the road, down at its very depths, where the houses knitted into one another like the links on an Aran sweater. He could not believe that so many people lived in so many houses. He could not believe how they tumbled out of their houses on a Sunday morning, grandparents, parents, children, grandchildren, a tide of old and young, all swimming together towards the chapel.

There had been so many masses on Sunday in those days, and so many priests to say them, but, even so, he wondered looking at them how they could cope. The kindly parish priest, Father Arthurs, sensed his anxiety. 'It is some sight, isn't it? Put your trust in the Lord. You will be fine.'

So, he put his trust in the Lord and began his journey; that long march of faith that had not yet been completed. Every day brought another stumbling step. The mass had been in Latin in those days. He marvelled as the congregation had unpacked their prayer books and read the mass with him, following him in English as he spoke Latin. The language came easily to him and he thought it incredible that, all over the world, in Europe, Africa, Asia and in the Americas, prayer communities like theirs were coming together, led by priests like him, listening to the mass in Latin, united in one common language, praying to God.

He had liked that aspect of the mass and had always been a little sorry that the changes of Vatican II had done away with Latin entirely. Surely, he thought, we could have kept the opening blessing in Latin, as a little reminder of the past and a nod to the present, that the Church was, in fact, universal?

It suddenly occurred to him that he had not spoken Latin in many decades. Goodness, he thought, yes, decades. What would the young ones think of it now if you were to tell them that their grandparents were Latin speakers? He laughed; they would not believe it. They would not believe that the language of Julius Caesar lived on the tongue of the city's Catholics.

Another loss, he thought, another retreat. The language, like the public processions, had faded from memory now. What had once been instinctive and welcomed was now hesitant and unwelcomed. The Corpus Christi procession had been reduced to a handful of the faithful, both proud and pitiful, he thought. The onlookers gawped in ignorance as they watched them process down the road. You could hear them ask each other, 'What's that about?'

They had swung from rules for everything, to rules for nothing. Still, those who marched, those who answered the call, were good people. They had faith and their company comforted them. They were still standing. That was something in this day and age.

Latin! He laughed again. He had swapped Latin for Irish. The locals had set up a little Irish-language primary school in the parish, a bunscoil. The head had approached him cautiously and asked if he could say mass for them in Irish or if he knew of a priest who might. 'Some of the teachers and parents would like that.'

'Some?' he thought. He registered the number; some, not all.

'Goodness,' he said. 'My Irish is very poor.'

'Of course,' said the head, waiting for a refusal.

He was suddenly gripped by an urge to prove his linguistic credentials. 'Do you know my grandmother, a McKendry from the Glens, was a native speaker of Irish?'

'Really?'

'Oh, yes. People forget that there used to be native speakers here, before partition. I remember her speaking Irish with my grandfather and some others. They had a very small farm. Farm, I say, a holding really. A few sheep, you know. She was born, if I remember correctly, around 1870, twenty years after the Great Famine. Hard to credit.'

The head warmed to him and he to her. He pushed 'some' from his mind. They began to talk about languages and their importance. They found out that they had been to the same Gaeltacht college in Donegal and swapped stories about the courses they had been on and staff that had been there.

Finally, the conversation paused.

'So,' said the head, 'about that mass ...'

'Yes,' said the priest, 'I will give it a go. I won't be able to give a homily in Irish, you know, but no one will miss that.'

The head laughed. A little too quickly, he thought.

'However,' said the priest, 'I should be able to do the rest. I will have to practise but it should not be beyond me.'

'*Maith an fear*,' said the head.

'Well, don't say that until you have heard my *droch-Ghaeilge*.'

They both laughed, set a date for the mass and shook hands. It seemed to the priest that he had no sooner made the promise to say mass in Irish than the day arrived. A few staff, some parents and a handful of pupils gathered together in the makeshift dining hall. The children were so young, thought the priest. He offered up a prayer in his head, in English, to the Holy Spirit that He might inspire the gift of tongues in him and began, '*In ainm an Athar agus an Mhic ...*'

Latin fell away, the world fell away, time hurtled backwards. He was with his grandparents again, on a hillside in the Glens. His grandmother was calling to him. It was such a long time ago. He hears only one word, '*bainne*'. She has *bainne* for him; he must bring the *bainne* up to his parents. *Bainne. Bainne. Bainne.*

So, he thought, afterwards as they gathered around for a cup of tea and he poured *bainne* into his cup, the Holy Spirit did hear my prayer. I have swapped Latin for Irish. He could not help but be moved by the occasion and by those who stood before him. They came to him, shook his hand and spoke to him in fluent Irish. He nodded, answered as best he could, reached for words that had long since buried themselves in forgetfulness. He stuttered '*go raibh maith agat, go raibh maith agat*' and remembered his *bean an tí* in Donegal, warm bread, jam and butter sitting on the table for supper. '*Go raibh maith agat, a bhean an tí.*'

Those poor people in the Gaeltacht, what they had to put up with, he thought.

His efforts seemed to satisfy them. They smiled; he smiled; the children smiled. What was the Irish for smile, he wondered, I will have to look it up. The head came up to him at the end and spoke, thankfully, in English. 'That was wonderful. You did us proud.'

He welcomed the flattery. 'Well, I don't know but I did my best.'

'It was wonderful.'

He walked out into the sunshine and looked at the prefabs that were being used for classrooms. This must have been what it was like for Colm Cille on Iona, he thought. Yes, he thought, they are, in their own way, founding a monastery, a centre of learning. I should go to Iona, he thought, take the boat across to Scotland and drive up. I should do that. He looked up at the mountain, brooding above. The Irish for mountain is '*sliabh*' he remembered, re-remembered. That seemed appropriate too, a mountain above the people, he thought, a reminder of Sinai and God's presence in the world. I must mention that in a sermon, he thought, I must link the physical and the metaphysical together; mountain and lore, language and place. *Sliabh,* he said aloud, *sliaabbhh.*

He marvelled as Irish began to bloom like wild flowers on the city's streets, just as American programmes became more popular. When he began his ministry, the girls would be baptised after saints and called Agnes and Margaret and Katherine and Mary, and the boys Michael and John and James. Now, the girls' names moved between Aisling and Kylie and the boys between Dónal and Jordan. Names in Irish had been uncommon in his youth. His brother was 'Séamus' to all but was called 'James' on his birth certificate because the registrar – an Orangeman – had refused point blank to accept Séamus as a 'proper name for any child in Northern Ireland'. The Orangeman had gotten his way too. James he was, officially, and when he was feeling mischievous he would tell visiting American relatives 'Séamus is my rebel name.' That was how things were then. He wondered what that Orangeman might make of all the uppity Catholics and their Irish names now?

He glanced at his watch once more. Time enough still. By rights the wedding was not his responsibility. The curate should officiate but the curate was not feeling well and the Monsignor had decided on one final act of charity towards the young man. 'I'll take that wedding. You rest up,' he had told him the night before.

'Are you sure, Monsignor?' said the curate with no real sincerity.

'Yes. You rest up. You have a lifetime of weddings before you. I'll do this last one. Give me the details and I'll take it from there.'

'Thank you, Monsignor,' the curate replied. The Monsignor just nodded and left. A lifetime of weddings? He realised that he was being uncharitable and doubted whether the curate would manage a lifetime of weddings.

The curate would probably not manage more than a few years as a priest. The Monsignor had heard the stories and had seen the curate at work; the curate was too soft, too brittle for his vocation. It was a shame, thought the Monsignor. It wasn't that the curate was a bad sort; he just didn't seem to have the necessary hard edge that was needed. Grit, you need a bit of grit. Questions were all very well but there came a time when you just had to bow your head, free yourself from doubt and let yourself go into God's journey. What was that parting blessing they had in Mexico? *Vaya con Dios*. Go with God. Yes, that was it. *Vaya con Dios*. He had gone with God.

He remembered again his own years as a curate. The Bishop had sent him to the city as soon as he was ordained. He had not wanted that. He should have complained to the Bishop that he was a country boy and there were plenty of parishes up in the north of the county where he would happily serve. But you did not complain to the Bishop then. No one complained to the Bishop. He had given a vow of obedience, and obedient he would be. That had not been as easy as he had thought but he managed. He emptied himself in the sacrifice of the mass, wrote his homilies with care, prepared for baptisms, weddings and funerals with great consideration. He quickly gained a reputation as being approachable amongst his parishioners. He was not a priest to instil fear, nor did he mind that. He saw no fear in his being a priest. He saw nothing but God and his vocation. He remembered his own ordination and his fellow priests laying their hands upon him. There were so many of them. He remembered thinking that he was surrounded; like he was caught up in a schoolyard game and that he was the last one to be caught at tig. He could still feel their hands upon him, could still remember their breath around him, hear the shuffle of feet as the older priests made towards him and the heat of their company as they drew him in. There had been so many of them; they had loved him and they were all gone now. He was the last of them, the last man standing. He felt the tiredness and sadness growing in his eyes and heart. He would not surrender to melancholy, not before a wedding. No. He breathed deeply, joined his hands in prayer, bent his head and sought Christ. His mind emptied of darkness and grew in light. He prayed. Yes. That was it. The sadness ebbed quickly. They had taken care of him, they had guided him, touched his soul and he had remained loyal to them. He had not faltered or, at least, when he had faltered, he had not fallen. He had kept good his promise, remained steady in his vocation. They would have been proud of him. They were proud of him. They had gone to their eternal rest and he had prayed for them in death as they had prayed for him in life. They had been his example and he had followed the best of them. There was no need for tears or regrets. He had been happy as a priest. He had done his best for his colleagues, defended the fellowship of priests, led by example, worked and nurtured his vocation and that of others.

Was that why the curate annoyed him so much? He had given so much over so many years and now, in his seventies, he was to retire from active ministry and return home, to leave the city and replant himself in the countryside of his youth. Was he failing the curate? Could he guide and help him more? He felt his hands tighten together. How much more could he offer? He had done everything in his power to lighten the curate's load, to help him along the way. He did not seek to suffocate or frighten the curate. He had allowed him as much freedom as he could; he had encouraged him to take extra courses; to come to him for advice when he wanted. What did the Americans call it? To be open. Yes. He had let the curate be open. It was more freedom than the Monsignor had been allowed. He had lived with parish priests who were little more than gaolers, who saw their curates as inmates, freed only to say mass and deliver the sacraments. He remembered them and his heart paused. Some of them had been too harsh. Did he appear like that to his own curate? No. He had tried to be fair. No, he had been fair. The curate could have no complaints. He felt anger mix with tiredness. This was not what he wanted, not before this wedding, the curate's wedding, the curate who was feeling poorly and who was tucked up in bed in the parochial house while he, in his seventies, prepared once more for another mass, while he, in his seventies, tried to preach to two eejits who would be better off not marrying at all. Oh, that curate. He was the young one, the spoilt one. He was the one who was to be protected and nannied because there were so few young men taking Holy Orders.

Harry had knocked gently on the door and put his head in.

'Need anything, Father?'

'No. All well. Any sign of movement out there?'

'Beginning to fill up,' said Harry. 'Word is that the groom will be here soon. It is probably bedlam at their house. They are already living together. You know that?'

'Right,' he had replied.

'It's not that unusual now,' said Harry.

'Right,' replied the Monsignor.

'They are not a bad pair.'

'Of course,' replied the Monsignor, 'at least there are no children.'

'Well, actually, he has one with another woman. A son. But he won't be there. The son, that is. The other woman will be looking after him.'

'Right,' said the Monsignor. He knew the score. All the fire and brimstone speeches of the last century had failed. The sexual revolution had won. At least they were marrying. At least they were doing that. He would pray for them, give them a mass they would not forget, he would storm heaven for them, he thought. Then he found himself adding a sour little aside – not that they would care.

The gloom gripped him again. Waste and disappointment wrapped itself around his soul. He breathed in again, deeply, closed his eyes again, went into his soul again to try and find some peace. He could no longer recognise himself. He felt on his worse days that he was nothing but a husk. On those days the prayers left him unmoved. On those days he felt his connection with God sundered. No. That was too dramatic. On those days he felt bereft, empty, alone.

He paused again, went deep within himself, prayed, sought out the Holy Spirit, waited. It has not been a waste, he said, you have done your best, he said, you have much to be thankful for, he said. He thought of his ministry, allowed himself a moment or two of pride in his achievements. He had lived as he had wanted to live. God had found him; he had answered God's invitation; he could have done nothing else. The path was clear, the path had been lit up by the Holy Spirit, he had been called; he had answered the call. That was as it should have been.

He had tried to make them more spiritual. He had seen the Protestant preachers in the city centre standing with their bibles and giving forth about the Lord. At first, he had been amused and a little embarrassed by their coarseness. It did not seem dignified to him, to stand there and shout about God and resurrection while the crowds milled around indifferently. Gradually, however, he saw courage in their ministry. They had to be brave men to stand up like that and bear witness in the public square, he realised, while embarrassed shoppers dipped their heads like swans on the river and carried on. It was more difficult for them than it was for him; his congregation sat mute and leaden before him week after week.

The spirit moved him. At one Sunday mass he cast aside his usual sober sermon and tried to imitate the evangelicals in the city centre; he tried to rouse the sheep from their stupor and to give them more than he had given until then, to spark their religious imagination, to show them that they were part of an ancient prayer community stretching back thousands of years into the Holy Land.

'We live in the shadow of a mountain. You all see the mountain every day as you go to work, or to the shops or to school. I want you to look more closely at the mountain every day. I want you to look at the mountain and to think of another mountain. I want you to look at the mountain and think of Mount Sinai and Moses standing at its peak. I want you to remember that God spoke to Moses on Mount Sinai, that God came down from heaven and that he spoke with Moses and gave him the Ten Commandments. God was on that mountain with him, and God is on our mountain with us. God speaks to us every day from our mountain, but we fail to listen. I want you to look at the mountain and listen for God's word coming from above. I want you to realise that God is always with us. We live in the shadow of a mountain and we live in the presence of God. Our mountain is Moses' mountain. We are an ancient people and Christianity is an ancient religion and our religion and our *Bible* has a tap root into Judaism and into an even more ancient prayer community. Remember this, every time you pray in the shadow of the mountain, you pray with Moses on his mountain. Never forget that. Never forget how ancient this faith of ours is. Never forget that it has endured despite dungeon, fire and sword, and in spite of our own failings. We pray here today, in this lovely church, in the shadow of the mountain, on this ancient island on the edge of Europe, but we stretch back across thousands of years and thousands of miles and our first home, our first spiritual home, is in Jerusalem and the

Holy Land and the deserts of far away lands. Never forget …'

He let himself go from the pulpit. He cast aside his usual reticence; he cast aside all that was sober in him and thought of himself down the town, preaching above the people as they shuffled from shop to shop, fearful in their poverty and frightened of the bombs that smashed flesh and bone. He let himself go. He wanted them to know God personally; he wanted them to know God spiritually. Following the rules was not enough; turning up was not enough. He wanted them to know God urgently; he wanted them to know how close to God they were. He let himself go.

He remembered that Sunday well. He did not judge it a success. He could see the congregation before him looking confused and bemused. He could hear the sour humour. 'Moses? Who is this fellow Moses? Is he the fellow who lives down the road?'

He could have sworn that he heard the Bishop, long dead, whisper in his ear after that homily. 'We don't have need of intellectuals here. Keep it simple for a simple people.'

No, he thought, I will not be remembered for my sermons. If I am remembered at all, it will be because I was charitable, understanding. I turned the other cheek, had given and sought no reward. I have been loyal to the church and dedicated to my parishioners. Still, it would have been nice to write a book, just one book.

Over the years though, his labours had not gone unnoticed. The church had made him a Monsignor in recognition of his devotion.

'A promotion then, Father,' said Harry all those years ago.

'Yes,' he had replied.

'They will be sending you up to the Bishop's Palace soon,' said Harry.

'God forbid!' he said, and they both laughed.

They had made him a Monsignor – though most of his parishioners continued to call him 'Father'. He had, at first, tried to coax them into using the title but grew tired of their blank questions. 'What's the difference, Father?' He had explained but grew tired of that and accepted whatever title they felt fit to bestow. 'Be humble,' he said.

No, he would not have wanted to be a Bishop. No. He did not want that. God had been good to him – he did not give him that cross to bear or any other. He had kept his vows.

He had been accosted while on a trip to Dublin; a few youths screaming at him, 'You're a pervert! You're a pervert!' He had hurried on, turned away in terror and walked past them as quickly as he could. He had always hated Dublin. His parents would say openly, 'They betrayed us down in Dublin, abandoned us.'

He knew of no one who did not think the same, and it had always coloured his feelings towards it. He enjoyed the day trips south as it was a release from the daily grind and threat of home. He enjoyed visiting the National Gallery of Ireland, sitting in the National Library of Ireland, eating his sandwiches by the cricket pitch in Trinity College. Yes, it was nice, but he never loved Dublin. His father's description of the place always stuck in his mind. 'A brothel for the British army for four hundred years.'

He remembered his mother pursing her lips when she heard the word 'brothel'. She was caught between laughter and discomfort at the word. She did not disagree with the sentiment though. After the incident, he visited less and less and, when he did, he wore a scarf to hide his collar.

There had been temptations, though. He remembered during the heatwave of 1976 when the women of the city, under the ferocious sun, had begun to cast off their clothes and show off their white curves. They abandoned their traditional modesty, lay in their little gardens like it was Saint Tropez and walked down the streets in the flimsiest of outfits. He had watched them carefully and had thought, briefly, about saying something at mass. He decided against it in the end. They would think he was a pervert for noticing their white and pink mounds. He had been young enough then to notice them, and young enough to want to notice as they all baked together.

That was such a long time ago, he thought.

He opened his eyes, startled. It was Harry, showing all his age. 'Old age has nothing to recommend it,' his father had said to him as he lay dying. Harry and he were proof of that. 'The groom is here,' said Harry, 'he is outside getting some photos taken. No sign of the bride yet. It will probably be a while. The wee lassies like to make a big entrance these days.'

'Thanks, Harry,' he said.

His heart sank. Please, please God, do not let this be one of those Barbie doll weddings, he said. Please, please Holy Spirit, descend and light up this day with your presence. Please, if it is your will, let this be a sacred day and not profane. He closed his eyes again and sought out another prayer. He would go out to greet the groom in a while. Not yet. Not yet. He had to find his balance once again. Why had he agreed to this? He was too soft on the curate. He should have insisted that the curate carry on. He was spoiling the curate, knowing full well that the curate would not last the pace. He did spoil him. He knew why but never spoke the reason aloud. He did not want to leave the parish without a priest. The curate was all that stood between him and a happy retirement. With the curate here, he could go home with this head held high. He could leave his parishioners with a priest. He could do that one last thing for them. Despite everything, he would be able to boast that he had left a priest behind him. That was something in this day and age; that was no mean feat. So what if the curate was lazy and undisciplined and spoilt? He was a priest. He was ordained. He would carry on the work. He would learn. Yes, he would learn.

Harry was at the door again. 'You'll never believe it, but the bride is here on time. She is ready to come in.'

He could not resist the question. 'How does she look?'

'Very modest, believe it or not. I keep waiting for some bride to come down the aisle in a bikini but this one looks dead classy.'

He laughed. 'Harry, you're a laugh. A bikini. It could happen yet. That might be the one that the curate will have to deal with. Let her know I am ready.'

He stood up, straightened his vestments and sought one last prayer before going out on the altar.

The groom looked at him as if he were a policeman. 'Don't worry,' he said to the groom while shaking his hand. 'I'm not going to lift you.' The groom and best man laughed quietly, understanding the humour. 'He would prefer it if the peelers did lift him,' whispered the best man, and the three of them laughed lightly again, just before the organ blared out its opening notes.

Harry was right, he thought, the bride did look very classy. The dress was appropriate, the music just right. The Holy Spirit has been listening, he thought. Yes, the Holy Spirit was here, he thought. This will be a good day.

He looked at the bride again as she approached the altar, full of smiles as she recognised family and friends. Yes, she looked beautiful and the dress was modest, he thought. He blinked and felt himself grow dizzy. Old age has nothing to recommend it. The bride was in front of him. Her father shook hands with the groom and stood back. He had seen this scene so many times. He reached for the words of the opening blessing and felt himself empty. Where were the words? He could see the wedding party looking at him, someone stirred.

'Something is wrong,' he heard a voice from the pews say.

What is wrong, he thought. What is wrong?

He felt himself spinning and diving. Someone has clipped me from behind, he thought. Some dirty gaunch has clipped me with their hurl, he thought. He turned to see who it was and fell. He heard voices. A free. It must be a free, he thought. The crowd were calling for a free. He was on the ground, confused. Grass should not be this cold and hard, he thought. Something was wrong. Someone was holding his hand; it was a woman in white with soft, soft hands. It is my mother, he thought, what is my mother doing on the pitch? She should not be on the pitch. No, not my mother; the bride, he thought. It is the bride. What is the bride doing on the pitch? She will dirty her lovely white dress. She should get off the pitch. He tried to raise himself up and wave her away. He tried to speak, to warn her about the muddy pitch. They had gathered around him. He could feel hands fluttering around him and hear people breathing. There were so many of them. He was surrounded; like he was caught up in a schoolyard game and that he was the last one to be caught at tig. He could feel their hands upon him and feel their breath around him. He could hear the shuffle of feet as people made towards him and the heat of their company as they drew him in.

'It's alright, Monsignor,' said the bride. 'It's alright.'

He could feel her soft hands on his shoulders.

Yes, he thought, yes, Monsignor. I am a Monsignor.

One more day in the vineyard, please Lord, one more day in the vineyard. Do not let my earthly journey end here; leave me one more day, if it is your wish. His breath deepened.

'Help me up,' he said to the groom.

The groom bent down towards him; his hands were rougher than the bride's, hardened by work before his time. He felt the groom's knotted skin in his own soft palm.

'Are you sure?' the groom asked.

'Yes, help me up. Please.'

The groom lifted him gently upwards.

The bride smiled. 'Are you alright? You gave us a fright.'

About the Author

Pól Ó Muirí was born in Belfast and was educated at Saint Mary's Christian Brothers' Grammar School and Queen's University, Belfast, where he undertook degrees in Celtic Studies and Scholastic Philosophy. A writer and journalist, he was written in both Irish and English over many years and in various genres; including poetry, short stories, biography, radio drama and fiction for adult learners of Irish.